THE SPY

KING'S SECURITY

A. RIVERS

*To every woman who's lost it all
and risen from the ashes.*

1

———

FIONA

"FIONA, CAN YOU COME OUT TO RECEPTION, PLEASE? THE police are here to see you."

I frowned and glanced up from my computer. Stephanie, who worked at the front desk, was hovering in front of me, her face scrunched with apprehension—whether from interrupting me or because of the police's presence, I wasn't sure.

"Is it Detective Lee?"

My boss, Ronan King, the chief executive of King's Security, often liaised with the Chicago police via Detective Joanna Lee.

"No, it's not Joanna. I would have just let her through. It's a man and a woman I haven't met before." Stephanie grimaced. "I asked why they want to see you, but they said it's confidential. Sorry I can't be more helpful."

"It's not your fault." I stood and smoothed the front of my pencil skirt. "I suppose I'd better see what they're here for."

Stephanie's face softened with relief. "Thanks, Fi."

I sent her a reassuring smile. Dealing with the police could be intimidating. I didn't have the best history with them, so it had been difficult for me when I started as Ronan's assistant. Eventually, I'd gotten used to it, and Joanna was always good to deal with. Polite, professional, and only pushy when she felt it was warranted. Other cops still made me nervous.

We strode down the corridor together. I held the door open for her and then followed her into the spacious reception area. High-end artwork hung on the walls and I took a moment to appreciate my favorite—an abstract painting of the ocean in shades of blue, purple, and green—before focusing on the police seated on the designer sofa. Even without uniforms, it was obvious who they were. There was just something about the way a cop dressed and carried themselves that gave them away. Stephanie returned to her seat behind the desk while I made my way to them.

"Hello." I greeted them with a smile. "What can I do for you?"

They stood, and the woman brushed lint off her dark slacks.

"Fiona Ryan?" she asked.

"Yes." I nodded, the back of my neck prickling. For some reason, I had a bad feeling about this. Perhaps it was the way she appraised me as if determining whether I was a flight risk.

"I'm Detective Gloria Harrison and this is my partner, Detective Mark Goodwin. We'd like you to come down to the station so we can ask you some questions."

Internal alarms blared in my head. That wasn't the usual protocol for dealings between King's Security and the Metro P.D.

I forced my expression to remain neutral. "Can I ask what this is about?"

"We'd like to discuss an incident that occurred last night." She glanced around. "We'd prefer not to get into detail until we're somewhere more private."

"I can find a meeting room for us to use," I suggested. My instincts were warning me that going with them wouldn't be wise.

The male cop, Goodwin, put his hand on his hip. "With all due respect, Miss Ryan, we'd prefer to talk to you at the station."

My mouth went dry. Something was definitely off about this. "Is this regarding a King's Security matter? If so, you'd be better off speaking to one of the directors."

Harrison's lips firmed. "It's not."

That's what I'd been afraid of.

I drew in a slow, shaky breath. It seemed my past might be coming back to bite me in the ass. Again. "Can you call Detective Lee? I'd like to speak to her before I go anywhere."

Joanna was sensible. She knew me. Surely, she'd be able to help. But Harrison shook her head.

"Detective Lee is homicide," she said. "She's not in our unit, and she isn't relevant to this discussion."

My heart sped up. It felt as if it was pounding against the inside of my rib cage. A sense of déjà vu swept over me. Once again, the police had come for me, and once again, I was in the dark as to why. Last time, I'd lost my job, my reputation, my boyfriend, and all of my savings. I'd had to start over. Would this time be the same?

No. It couldn't. I had resources available to help me. I wouldn't let history repeat itself.

"I'll come with you. Just let me notify my boss that I'm leaving the office."

Harrison nodded her assent. I went to the reception

desk, her sharp eyes following me. I wouldn't go and speak to Ronan in person because I feared they'd insist on accompanying me, and that would create a stir in the office. At least out here there were fewer people to witness my humiliation. I leaned over the desk and spoke softly.

"Stephanie, can you please get Mr. King on the phone?"

She nodded, her eyes wide. "Of course." She dialed the extension for Ronan's office and waited for a moment. "Mr. King? I have Fiona on the line for you." Another pause. I could imagine Ronan would be confused. After all, I was usually the one patching calls through to him, not asking to be put through. "Yes, sir." She handed me the phone.

"Hi," I said, glancing back at the cops and lowering my voice. "I hate to ask, but would you be able to do me a favor?"

"What favor is that?" He sounded bemused.

"Can you please call my attorney and ask her to get to the Metro Police Station as quickly as possible?" I carried on without giving him a chance to respond. "Her name is Ariadne Rodgers. She works at MacBeth and Travers."

"Of course." I heard papers shuffling and hoped he was recording her details. "What's going on?"

"I'm not sure yet." I hesitated, then added, "It could be about those paintings. I don't want to take any risks."

"Would you like me to come and speak to them?" His tone was brusque. "I'm sure we can clear this up."

"Just get Ariadne down to the police station ASAP." It was nice to know Ronan had my back, but I didn't want to cause a scene. Although I was fully prepared to do so later if things went downhill.

"I will. And Fiona, if they make any accusations or ask questions you're unsure how to answer, stay quiet. Silence is always best."

"Thanks, Ronan." I'd learned that lesson myself as well

—the hard way. When you don't understand what's going on, it's easy to say things that can be used against you later, or to lose your temper and do or say something you regret. "Hopefully I'll be back soon."

"Be careful," he cautioned, and the phone disconnected. I passed it back to Stephanie and turned to face Detectives Harrison and Goodwin.

"Okay," I said, holding my head high. "Let me get my purse, and then we can go."

Thankfully, they didn't make a production of removing me from the building. After I ducked back to my desk for my purse, we left calmly. I got into the back of their car. They didn't speak during the drive—not to each other or to me—and when we arrived, I was ushered into an interview room.

"Do you mind if I record this conversation?" Detective Harrison asked, placing a voice recorder on the center of the table between us.

I cocked my head. "Do you need to read me my rights first?"

"You're not under arrest. I'd just like to be able to focus on our conversation now and take notes later."

"Okay," I allowed. I didn't intend on saying anything to incriminate myself, so surely it wouldn't hurt.

Harrison switched the device on, then leaned back in her chair and glanced at Goodwin, who rested his forearms on the table and watched me steadily.

"Where is the Monet?" he asked.

ZEKE

.   .   .

I was reviewing a report that Jonah had prepared on the communications between a prominent pharmaceutical mogul and his mistress when I noticed movement on the monitor for the camera feed connected to reception. A man and a woman were speaking with Fiona. Based on their appearance, I immediately picked them as cops. It wasn't unusual for us to work with the Met P.D.

I let my gaze linger, as it always did, on Fiona. My gut tightened. I'd wanted the sexy redhead from the moment she started working here, but nothing had happened between us for two reasons. First, she was one of our most valuable employees and Ronan would lose his shit if I did something to drive her away. Second, she didn't want a damn thing to do with me. I had no idea why, but she'd taken one look at me, scowled, and muttered something under her breath. Nothing I'd said or done since seemed to have thawed her.

I watched her stiffen as she spoke to the detective, and then cross to the front desk and talk on the phone for a minute or so. After she hung up, she left with them. I paused, rewound the footage, and zoomed in on her face. She looked anxious. I frowned. I couldn't think of any good reason for the police to need Fiona to go with them. At least, not related to our work at King's Security.

I grabbed my mobile phone and called Joanna Lee, the detective we worked with most closely.

"Detective Lee," she answered briskly.

"Jo, it's Zeke Watts." She'd probably already seen the Caller ID, but better safe than sorry. "Two of your detectives just left our office with Fiona Ryan. Do you have any idea what that's about?"

"It's nothing to do with my unit," she said. "I can't give you any information."

"But do you know what they want with her?" I asked.

She sighed. "I can't tell you, Zeke. I'm sorry."

"Not even for a bottle of whiskey?"

"No." Her tone was firm. "But I'll do you the courtesy of pretending you didn't just try to bribe a police officer."

I grinned to myself. I'd known the offer wouldn't get me anywhere, but Joanna was painfully straitlaced and it was fun to rile her. "Thanks anyway, Jo."

I hung up before she could instruct me to address her by her title, then I pushed my chair back and headed for Ronan's office. He, Kade, and I were the directors and founders of King's Security, but while we each held a stake in the business, Ronan was the chief executive because it had been his brainchild and he was best suited to the job.

I knocked on his door and pushed it open. Usually, Fiona would be seated at her desk near the entrance, ready to grill me about why I wanted to interrupt her boss's precious time, but of course she wasn't there now.

"Zeke." Ronan was standing behind his massive wooden desk, a briefcase in his hand and his suit jacket folded neatly over his shoulder. "I wondered how long it would take for you to turn up."

"What's happening?" I asked, knowing he'd know what I was talking about.

"I'm not sure, but Fiona asked me to call her attorney and have her go to the police station. My best guess is it's something to do with those paintings."

"But that was years ago." Before Fiona started working for us, she'd lost her job as the assistant to the manager of an art gallery because they suspected she'd used her access to the gallery to steal three expensive paintings. She'd never been charged, but they'd put her through the wringer.

He shrugged. "I don't know what else it could be." He stepped out from behind the desk. "I'm going down there too. She'll need support."

I winked. "Will you throw your weight around?"

Ronan's name meant something in law enforcement circles and the ten zeros following the number on his bank balance didn't hurt either.

"For however much good it will do."

"I'll have my guys see what they can dig up," I said. "I'll call you if I find anything."

"Thanks."

I returned to the quadrant of the office where my tech security superstars—AKA hackers who tried really hard to toe the line of what's legal—were housed, while Ronan went the other way. I stopped in the center of the open-plan area and clapped to get my staff's attention.

"Urgent task," I called. "The police just took Fiona Ryan in—potentially for questioning—and I want to know why. Put aside everything else until you've got me an answer. If any clients call, patch them through to Benson to take a message."

Benson was my personal assistant, as efficient as Fiona and just as sassy, but fortunately, unlike her, he didn't hate my guts. There were several confused glances, and a few people's eyes lit up—either because of the new challenge or the possibility of getting their hands on gossip. My guys were the best in their field, but they absolutely loved sticking their noses into other people's business. It was part of what made them so good. Honestly, it was a trait that I shared.

I strode past Benson into my office, and flopped onto my chair. I opened a new search bar on my computer and started with the obvious: articles about the missing paintings from four years ago. There was nothing new on that front, so I checked for any thefts or big news in the art world in general, but except for a missing idol from a museum in Cairo, all seemed quiet.

I ran a few more searches, my frown deepening. The absence of information either meant the police were keeping a tight lid on whatever new information they had, or that they wanted to talk to Fiona about something else entirely. That seemed unlikely, but I knew from hard-earned experience that the obvious answer wasn't always the right one, so I dug into Fiona instead.

When Howard, one of my best former hackers, knocked on the door, I sat up straight at his expression.

"What is it?" I demanded.

"I think a Monet has been stolen." The words tumbled from his mouth excitedly. "The Windy City Gallery was supposed to be opening an exhibition of impressionist paintings last night, with a work called *Daisies* by Monet as the centerpiece. The exhibition was canceled at the last minute and chatter on the dark net is that it's because of a theft."

"Monet." I rubbed my chin, my fingers rasping over stubble. "How much do you think the painting would be worth?"

"Millions of dollars." He came closer, a gleam in his dark eyes. "Maybe tens of millions."

"Shit. And you think this has something to do with Fiona?" My mind worked quickly. The paintings Fiona had been accused of stealing were worth significantly less than that. A paltry ten thousand dollars per item. It would be a stretch for the police to believe she'd gone from that to a multimillion-dollar heist, but if they thought they'd found a connection between the crimes, it was certainly within the realm of possibility that they'd take her in for questioning.

"Find out as much as you can about it and email it to me," I told him. "Get Jonah to see if he can find any electronic evidence to show where Fiona was last night in case we need an alibi for her." I stood and grabbed my leather jacket. "I'm going to catch up with Ronan."

If this was about a stolen Monet, it was a hundred times more serious than we'd originally thought, and I needed to share as much information as I could with Ronan in person. I wanted to be there for Fiona too, even if it wouldn't neces-sarily put her mind at ease. What kind of mess had that difficult woman gotten herself into?

2

———

FIONA

"WHAT MONET?" I DEMANDED, LOOKING FROM DETECTIVE Goodwin to Detective Harrison in confusion.

"Don't play dumb." Goodwin leaned over the table, getting closer to me. He was obviously the bad cop in this scenario. "You stole a priceless Monet from the Windy City Gallery, and we want to know where it is."

My mouth dropped open. "You're out of your minds." I glanced at the voice recorder, reminding myself not to say anything they could consider verbal assault. "I didn't steal a Monet."

Holy crap. What would I do with a Monet? I mean, I loved to study them, but it would hardly look at home on the wall of my small apartment. Not that I'd be able to display a stolen painting anywhere, and I had nowhere to hide one. I didn't have any rented storage containers, just a closet with way too much already stuffed inside.

"Where were you last night?" Harrison asked.

"At home." Even to my own ears, it sounded weak. "I left

work at six, took the L home, and ate dinner while I watched *Cupcake Contest.*"

"Uh-huh." Harrison's expression was skeptical. "Was anyone with you?"

"No."

"What about during the day?" Goodwin asked.

"I was at work." I relaxed a little. At least that could be easily proved. "I didn't leave the building, and we have good security camera coverage. I'm sure they'll approve you reviewing the footage to confirm that I didn't leave."

"Hmph." Harrison shifted forward, mimicking Goodwin's position. Elbows on the table. Jaw set. Expression hard. "And before that?"

"I was at home, then got a coffee from Bean Bonanza and took the L to the office."

"Alone?"

"Yes." My teeth clenched. "Alone. Although I'm sure someone on the train would have seen me."

"Hmm."

I hated those stupid thinking noises. They were trying to unnerve me.

"So, you spent the night alone, took the subway to the office, spent the day there, returned home via the L and spent the evening alone?" Goodwin clarified.

"That's right." I felt like squirming but made myself be still. If I fidgeted, I'd look guilty, and I had nothing to hide. "Couldn't you check my phone's location history to show where I was? The GPS is enabled." I knew Zeke, the arrogant and infuriating director of cybersecurity at King's Security, would be able to have that data in minutes, so surely they could too.

Goodwin shrugged one shoulder. "All that proves is where your phone was, not where you were. You could have left it behind or loaned it to someone else."

My chest tightened. He made a good point. People generally went everywhere with their phones, but someone who intended to commit a crime would probably make sure there was no means of electronically tracking them. If I was actually the mastermind behind the theft, I'd probably have arranged for someone to take my phone and my credit card and use them in a different area of town from where the crime was occurring, to give myself an alibi.

"When was the last time you were inside the Windy City Gallery?" Harrison asked.

I opened my mouth to answer but then closed it again and took a breath. "I won't answer any more questions without my lawyer present."

They gave me matching looks that said they thought asking for an attorney looked guilty as hell, but last time I hadn't and I'd ended up spending a night in a holding cell because they'd still thought I was guilty anyway. I had no intention of letting that happen again.

Harrison pulled her phone out and checked the screen. "Looks like you're about to get your wish."

A moment later, the door flew open and Ariadne stormed into the room, a little over five feet and 90 pounds of furious Harvard-educated woman. She pulled out the chair beside me and sat, crossing her legs and glaring at the detectives.

"Have you been questioning my client?" she demanded.

"Only informally," Goodwin replied. "She isn't under arrest."

Ariadne glanced at the voice recorder. "Looks official to me."

Harrison pocketed the device. "That's just for my personal records. Miss Ryan gave permission."

"I did," I admitted, my face flushing when Ariadne arched an eyebrow at me.

"Well, permission is now revoked." She reached into the bag she'd dropped beside her chair and withdrew a notebook and a pen, then opened the book to a fresh page. "On what grounds have you brought my client in for questioning?"

Goodwin rolled his eyes. "It's just a conversation."

"I suggested talking at the office," I told Ariadne. "They refused."

"Uh-huh." She made a note in shorthand. "So, detectives?"

Harrison shifted on her seat, growing visibly nervous. "A Monet was discovered missing from the Windy City Gallery early yesterday evening. We'd like Miss Ryan to share any information she may have about that."

Ariadne pursed her lips. "And why do you believe Miss Ryan would have any relevant information?"

Hesitating, Harrison exchanged a look with Goodwin, then moistened her lips. "The theft has certain similarities to the Black Swan case from four years ago."

My stomach dropped. I'd expected as much, considering they'd dragged me in, but hearing it was still a blow.

"My client wasn't charged for that crime," Ariadne said.

Goodwin scoffed. "We've seen the case file. It was solid."

"Yet the district attorney's office decided there wasn't enough evidence to press charges."

I felt a swell of satisfaction at their matching hangdog expressions. "Have you talked to Bergen?" I asked them.

If the theft had similarities to the one that had upended my life four years ago, that's who I'd be looking at.

"We can't discuss an ongoing investigation with you," Harrison said.

"Isn't that exactly what you purport to be doing?" Ariadne asked. She folded her arms. "Do you intend to charge my client?"

"No," Harrison replied reluctantly.

"Is she free to go?"

"Yes," Goodwin ground out. "We're not holding her." He turned to me. "But we'll be at your door the instant we have enough evidence."

Ariadne stiffened. "Is that a threat?"

"Of course not," he said quickly.

"Come on." Ariadne stood, tucked her notebook back into her bag, and touched my shoulder. "We're getting out of here."

I got to my feet, surprised by how shaky my legs were. Ariadne yanked the door open and waved me through, ignoring the angry mutterings behind us.

"Thanks, Ari," I murmured as she steered me down the corridor.

In the waiting area, two men near the exit caught my attention. Zeke was slouching in a chair, looking at something on his phone. His black hair was messy, as if he'd run his hands through it, and he wore his ever-present leather jacket. He tapped his phone screen, his tattooed fingers moving agilely and light glinting off his chunky rings. Give him a cigar and he wouldn't have looked out of place backstage at a rock concert.

Part of me was surprised to see him there. It wasn't as if we were friends. But another part of me had expected it. After all, he never had been any good at minding his own business. Ronan stood nearby, reading a poster attached to the wall.

"Miss Ryan?"

I glanced over my shoulder at Detective Harrison, who'd called down the corridor. "Yes?"

"Don't leave town."

A gasp of indignation escaped me, but thankfully, it wasn't loud enough for anyone other than Ariadne to hear.

"Ignore them," Ariadne whispered.

"Easier said than done." I cleared my throat, which was thick with emotion. "Thank you so much for coming."

"Anytime." She flashed a tight smile at me. "Next time, don't say a word until I get here."

"I won't."

She glanced at the men by the door. "Are you okay if I leave you with them?"

"Yeah."

"Great." She gave me a quick hug. "I'll see you at our next spin class... if not sooner."

"See you there." I watched her leave, noting that Zeke had looked up from the screen and his dark eyes followed her. He probably thought he'd found his next bed-warmer. He seemed to take it as a challenge to charm every woman he met. I was sure plenty of them ended up beneath him.

"No orange jumpsuit?" he asked as I approached.

I ignored him. "You didn't have to come," I said to Ronan.

"Of course we did." He smiled, and the expression softened his stern features. The man was gorgeous, although it had only been since he got together with his fiancée, Willow Lennox, that he'd smoothed over some of his rougher edges. "We'll drive you home."

"No." I said it so quickly they both seemed startled. I winced. "I mean, you should take me back to the office. I have plenty of time to do more work today."

Ronan considered this. "Don't feel like you have to. You must need a bit of quiet to get your thoughts together."

That's exactly what I don't want.

There was no one to distract me at home. I didn't want to mull over everything that had gone wrong today, and the myriad ways this could mess up my life.

"I'd rather be at work."

Zeke rose from the chair. "Let Fifi be a workaholic if that's what she wants."

I narrowed my eyes. "My name isn't 'Fifi.'"

"Fifi" sounded like a dog.

He smirked. "Why not? It's cute. You're cute. It fits."

"Just no."

Ronan jerked his head toward the exit and we followed him out. It was a short walk to the car and I slumped onto the back seat, feeling more drained than I'd realized. When we arrived at King's Security, Ronan indicated for us to join him in his office. He sat at the collaboration table, Zeke sat opposite him, and I claimed the seat at Ronan's side, more out of habit than anything else. A good assistant was always at their boss's right hand.

"I'll call Kade," he said. A few minutes later, the last of the directors sauntered into the room, his broad shoulders nearly filling the doorway.

He came over to me. "How are you doing?"

I tried to look more put-together than I felt. "Been better, been worse."

He lowered his huge frame onto the chair closest to Zeke. "Run us through everything that's happened."

I glanced between them, suddenly feeling intimidated. Except for Zeke, these men had never been anything but kind to me yet, for some reason, I hated the thought of unloading my baggage on them. I worked my ass off to be excellent at my job. Their respect meant something to me. I didn't want to lose it.

ZEKE

· · ·

Fiona was too pale. I didn't like it.

Even though she was a classic redhead, with richly colored hair and alabaster skin—except for the smattering of freckles across her nose—she always seemed vibrant. Now, she was wan, and it was wrong. Fiona should be filled with life, not slumped with defeat. I was tempted to tease her just to put some color back in her cheeks, but she'd had a tough day already. She didn't need me to behave like an ass.

"Go on," I said gently.

She looked at me with surprise but then nodded. "Um, so you all know the story behind what happened before I came to work here."

"You were accused of stealing three paintings from the gallery where you worked," Ronan said. "The paintings were replaced with forged copies so no one could be sure exactly when they were taken, but yours was the only key card used outside of normal working hours, and your credit card had recently been used to buy canvases of that size, as well as paints and other supplies from a local store."

Fiona cleared her throat. "Yeah, that's about it. I swear I didn't do it, though."

"We know," Ronan said. "Do you think I would have hired you if I thought you were a thief?"

I noticed some of the tension ease from her shoulders.

"So, what we need to know is, what actually happened?" Kade asked. "Ronan never pressed at the time he hired you. He was satisfied with the report by the private detective we hired, which concluded the same thing the police did: that there wasn't enough evidence to press charges. Given the state of your finances and your lack of contact with any known fences, he thought it was unlikely you were behind the thefts."

Fiona's cheeks flushed red, and I felt a pang of sympathy.

It was never nice to talk about being broke—especially to people who had plenty of money in the bank.

"It's actually really simple," she said, her voice unwavering. "My ex-boyfriend screwed me over."

My gut flipped. Whatever I'd expected her to say, it wasn't that. My fingers curled into fists. "What did he do?"

Her eyes flicked to me and then lowered to the tabletop as if it was easier to get the words out that way. "I was an artist in addition to being assistant to the gallery manager," she said. "That's why they were so suspicious of the purchases. They thought I could have painted the forgeries. I wasn't that talented. Not that they believed me." She intertwined her slender fingers and stared down at them. "My boyfriend was skilled enough to have forged them, though. I was financially supporting Bergen while he worked on his art. He was good, and I thought he had a chance of making it big one day." She sighed. "Keep in mind that I don't know any of this for certain, but my guess is that Bergen painted the forgeries, then took my key card while I was sleeping and swapped the forgeries out for the originals." Her mouth curled downward. "All I know for sure is that when I got back from being questioned by the police, he was gone from the apartment, my credit cards had been maxed out, and he'd emptied our joint bank account."

"Son of a bitch," Kade growled. The former soldier had a chip on his shoulder when it came to men hurting or taking advantage of women. Often, I teased him for having a white knight complex, but this time, I wholeheartedly agreed.

"What the fuck kind of name is 'Bergen' anyway?" I asked.

Fiona rolled her eyes. "I thought it was unique. I was stupid."

I wanted to argue that she hadn't been stupid. I knew how much a betrayal could come out of the blue. I'd trusted my team at the secretive government agency I used to work for, first as a cyber specialist and then as an undercover operative, until I'd been set up to look like a traitor and subjected to their "advanced interrogation techniques"—AKA torture. For an instant, the memory made it difficult to draw a breath. My vision darkened and I inhaled sharply, but then, thankfully, the sensation stopped.

"Did the police find any evidence to connect him to the theft?" I asked.

"No." She shook her head in disgust. "He supposedly had an alibi. He claimed to have been spending the nights with another woman. I don't know who it was, but she backed him up. They both said he and I had already been broken up for a while and that I was trying to pin it on him out of spite because he left me for someone else."

My nostrils flared. "He thought a lot of himself, didn't he?"

I could tell from the way she looked like she'd tasted something sour that it pissed her off to have to admit this to us. I got it. Not only did it make her look like a vindictive ex-girlfriend, but a woman like Fiona wouldn't be used to men leaving her. She was gorgeous, smart-mouthed, and intelligent. Hell, if I had a chance to taste her fire, I'd never let her get away.

"They believed him," she said. "They didn't have enough to charge me, but I lost pretty much everything anyway."

3

————

FIONA

"That won't happen again," Kade said grimly. "We won't let it."

A thread of hope curled in my gut. "You believe me?"

"I sure as hell do." He nodded toward Ronan. "You already know Ronan does. Even if I had any doubts, the fact that you came into work today would cinch it. What kind of person would show up to the office the day after stealing a priceless Monet?"

I turned to Zeke. He'd always been the one who was more suspicious and cynical of people's motives. "What about you?"

His lips quirked. "I disagree with Kade on that last point. A great thief would go about their routine as normal regardless of what they'd been up to. What better way to look innocent than to act as though nothing had happened?"

Angry heat simmered inside me and I narrowed my eyes at him. "But—"

"You didn't let me finish." He smirked. Damn, I wanted

to wipe that annoying expression off his face. "I don't think you are a thief. I was just pointing out what the police's perspective might be. Your being here today is a good bluff. That said, you obviously didn't do it, and we can't afford to lose the boss's right-hand woman, so I guess we'll just have to prove your innocence."

"W-what?" I couldn't believe my ears. Surely Zeke, the most frustrating man I'd ever had the displeasure of working with, hadn't just suggested coming to my rescue.

"He's right." Ronan sighed and ran a hand over his tidy hair. "The best way to beat this is to be proactive. We need to either prove you can't have done it by locking down your alibi, or find who actually stole the Monet."

I blinked at them in shock, momentarily speechless. "You'd do that for me?"

"Of course we would," Kade said gruffly.

"But it shouldn't be your problem. It's not fair of me to expect you to help me clean up my own mess. Especially since you were already generous enough to give me this job despite my history." Ronan had taken a chance on me when no one in my old circles would. I didn't want to repay him by making his life more difficult.

Ronan stacked his hands one on top of the other on the table. "You're family to us, and we take care of our own. We're helping you."

My lower lip wobbled. My throat constricted and I blinked rapidly to stop the tears that were welling in my eyes from spilling over. "Thank you."

"Great. That's decided." Zeke clasped his hands together. "Moving on. It seems to me that considering the nature of the crime, our best bet is to look for electronic evidence. I'll take the lead."

My stomach fluttered. *Zeke* would be the one trying to clear my name? I didn't know how to feel about that. On one hand, he was excellent at what he did, but on the other, he never seemed to take anything seriously. Did I really want to rely on him for something so important?

"You'll make this your top priority?" Ronan asked.

"Sure. It'll be like an electronic game of Clue. The guys will love it."

The fluttering turned into nausea.

"Can't you take something seriously for once?" I snapped. "This is my life."

Zeke's crooked smile didn't waver. "I take it very seriously, Fifi, and my team will too. They work harder when we make it fun or give them something to compete over. Trust me."

My stomach sank. That was the whole problem. I *didn't* trust him.

I had no particular reason not to. I knew his reputation as being the best in his field, and we had a long list of satisfied clients because of him. But I had a difficult time seeing him as an expert cyber specialist rather than as the devil-may-care flirt he'd become whenever we were in the same room. Beyond that, the truth was, I didn't really trust anyone. After all, I'd trusted Bergen, and look where that had gotten me.

"Surely we don't need you *and* your team working on it," I said, my thoughts again returning to the huge mountain of crap I'd dumped at my boss's feet. "I don't want to cause any issues with meeting deadlines for other projects. I could just work closely with one of your people."

Zeke's grin widened. "Nice try, sweetheart, but you're not getting out of working with me. You're a V.I.P. That means you get the white glove service."

Despite my reservations, I warmed at the thought that Zeke considered me important. It had never occurred to me that he might see me as more than a challenge to his lady-killer reputation.

I turned to Ronan. "Is that a good idea? I'd hate to be responsible for problems with paying clients."

I couldn't afford to pay for their time. I knew the rates these guys charged out at and they weren't even in my ballpark. The only reason I could afford Ariadne as my attorney was because I'd known her since school and she gave me a heavy discount.

"Zeke knows what his team are and are not capable of," Ronan said with a shrug. "If he thinks they can handle this without dropping any balls, then that's his call."

I met Zeke's eyes. They were so dark they were nearly black, but when I took the time to look past the attitude he wore like a shield, I saw a hint of real emotion in them. For whatever reason, he did care.

"Thank you," I said thickly. "Thank you all."

"It's no problem." Ronan pushed his chair back. "Call a temp to cover for you. You can focus on yourself until everything is cleared up."

I pressed my lips together. He was an amazing boss, and I'd never take it for granted. "Thank you."

Zeke rolled his eyes. "Stop thanking him and let's get started. Come with me."

He stood and stretched, his shirt riding up to reveal an inch of tattooed abdomen. I tore my gaze away from that intriguing patch of skin just in time for him to notice. His expression turned smug but he didn't mention it, instead sauntering out of the office as if he didn't have a care in the world. I thanked Ronan and Kade again, excused myself, and placed a call to the temp agency we used. Once that was done, I went to Zeke's office and knocked softly.

He glanced up from his computer, a pair of glasses perched on the end of his nose that somehow only made him sexier. "You know, you didn't have to manufacture this whole situation just to spend more time with me," he teased. "You could have asked."

I snorted. Perfect. There was the reminder I needed about exactly who he was. Sarcastic. Flirtatious. Not the kind of man I should ever be attracted to.

***

ZEKE

WITH BALANCE RESTORED, I OPEN A SEARCH TAB ON MY computer. For a few seconds there, Fiona had been looking at me in a way I didn't understand, and I'd had to get us back on an even footing.

"Grab a chair and pull it up," I told her.

The first order of business was to look into her asshole ex. A subtle floral scent tickled my nostrils as she parked a chair a couple of feet away and perched primly atop it, her thighs crossed and her skirt pulled tight across them. I forced myself not to stare. She made a tempting picture.

"What's Burger's last name?" I asked.

"Bergen," she corrected. "It's Cole."

"Bergen Cole," I said, typing it into the search field. It was a unique enough name that I doubted I'd need to add many filters before I found who I was looking for. Sure enough, I found a social media account right away, along with a Wikipedia page for Bergen Cole, Artist. I skimmed the wiki page. It was basic, with a few sentences about his life and a list of his known works. I exited the page and opened the social media account. Images of landscape paintings filled the screen. Mountains, streams, skylines, and several of a flower garden. I didn't have much of an eye for art, but I could tell he was reasonably talented.

I scrolled down the page until I found a photograph of a person I assumed was Bergen. My hand froze on the mouse and my eyebrow popped up. The man in the photograph had dark, shaggy hair, brown eyes, harsh features, tattoos climbing the sides of his neck, and a cocky smirk. In short, he looked so similar to me that we could have been brothers.

"Shit." I whistled. "I'm totally your type."

"Are not," she retorted.

I glanced at the screen pointedly.

Her cheeks turned pink. "Okay, so there's a resemblance, but did you ever stop to think that maybe that's exactly what makes you *not* my type?"

I frowned and waited for her to elaborate.

She huffed. "What person would want to go out with someone who reminded them of the worst time of their life?"

Ouch. I rubbed my chest. Now that she said it, I could see her point. Being around me must be difficult sometimes. A constant reminder of what she'd been through. Was this why she'd disliked me on sight? If so, it would explain a lot. Still, it would be nice to be seen as my own person. I didn't like being lumped in with someone else and paying for their sins.

Also, what were the odds? When I left my job at the agency, half the reason I covered myself with tattoos and got damn near everything pierced was to make myself as recognizable as possible, so I could never be used as a nameless, faceless tool again. The chance of finding someone who resembled me so closely must be infinitesimal, but apparently, not impossible.

"Got it." I clicked out of the social media page and

opened a website that appeared to be dedicated to Bergen Cole and his art.

Beside me, Fiona sighed. "I'm sorry. I didn't mean to be rude. It's just been a long day."

"I understand. We're good." I shouldn't be teasing her anyway. It would be best for me to just focus on the task at hand. Perhaps I should lay off flirting with her in general. I enjoyed seeing her bristle and blush, but if it was causing her genuine distress, that wasn't okay. "Tell me more about Bergen. Is he from Chicago?"

"Yes," she replied. "At least, that's what he told me."

I glanced at her. "I don't suppose you know his social security number."

She rolled her pretty eyes. "No, Zeke. I don't make it a habit to learn my boyfriends' social security numbers."

I didn't point out that it might be a good habit to start.

"What about his year of birth?"

She gave it.

I mentally did the math. "So he's thirty-five?"

"That sounds about right. He was thirty when we started dating, and we were together for a bit more than a year."

The age also meshed with his photograph from social media. I opened the site again, copied the image and ran a reverse search to see if I could find it—or him—elsewhere. Several websites popped up. Most of them were from art galleries or blogs, with a couple of interviews in online magazines. I opened one of them and scanned the text. It was full of self-congratulatory bullshit.

"He sounds like a self-entitled douche," I said.

"He is." She didn't sound mad. Just resigned. "That's the kind of man I generally attract."

Double ouch. I'd been flirting with her for years. Had she meant that as a slight against me or had she just not thought before she spoke?

"Did he work at all while you were together?"

"Only on his art."

"And he's strictly a painter?"

She waved her hand back and forth. "He dabbled in sculpture but he was never as good at it as he was at painting."

"Does he have family? Do you know if he's still in the city?" The more information I had, the better the instructions I could give my team.

"He has a mom who worships the ground he walks on. She didn't have a husband and I'm not sure what the deal with Bergen's dad was. He never told me. I'm not sure if he even knows him."

"Siblings?"

She laughed dryly. "None. Lucky, because he'd never have been able to stand having his mom's attention divided."

"So, he's a momma's boy?"

"Only in that he adores her because she dotes on him. It's good for his ego."

"Right." The more I learned about this guy, the worse he sounded. "Close friends?"

She scowled. "He makes friends easily but doesn't keep them for long. In hindsight, that should have been a red flag. He always said they were jealous of him, and I bought it."

"Jesus, Fi. How did you not see what a tool this guy was?"

She closed her eyes and buried her face in her hands, releasing a muffled growl. When she raised her face again, she looked so sad I wanted to pull her into my arms and hold her.

"I was blind, and apparently, the police are too. When you figure out how to fix that, let me know. I'd really appreciate it."

4

FIONA

After Zeke finished pulling together a basic information bundle about Bergen, he shifted to looking for details about the crime itself.

"Which Monet was stolen?" I asked as he jotted notes on a tablet.

"*Daisies*," he replied.

I closed my eyes and summoned an image of the painting to mind. I'd familiarized myself with most of Monet's works during my studies. *Daisies* was a painting of a grassy hill speckled with tiny white and yellow flowers beneath a cloudy sky. Monet's works were famously grand in scale, but *Daisies* was on the smaller side, measuring approximately three feet in length and two feet in height. He'd painted it not long after completing his iconic *Water Lilies* collection. It wasn't as well-known as his most famous works, but it would still be worth upward of five million dollars, assuming the person who'd stolen it knew a decent fence. Without someone to connect them with a buyer, it was essentially worthless.

"We have to assume Bergen already has a fence lined up," I said. "He never got caught with the paintings four years ago, and he was very money-focused so I doubt he'd have stolen them purely for the joy of having them, as other people might. He probably had a fence then, and if so, he'll be able to use them again now."

"Hmm." Zeke cocked his head. "I follow your logic but there's a difference between fencing a couple of lower valued paintings by a moderately well-known modern artist versus an original Monet. The fence he used back then might not have the right connections to get rid of a Monet."

"Maybe. But Bergen isn't reckless," I said. "He's manipulative and calculating. I didn't see it when we were dating, but I do in hindsight. I don't think he'd have stolen such a famous piece of art unless he had a plan."

"Assuming he did take it."

I flashed Zeke a look. "Assuming the crime was similar enough to the previous one for the police to come looking for me, then it must have been him or someone he shared his methods with."

"I'll grant you that."

I tapped my finger against my chin. "The painting was taken from the Windy City Gallery, right?"

He nodded.

"The woman who manages the gallery is an old friend of mine." Calling her a "friend" might be stretching the truth considering we hadn't been in touch since I was fired from my last job, but Patience was clever, and I didn't think she'd have believed I was guilty. "We should go and talk to her."

"I don't know if that's a great idea," Zeke warned. "Going to the gallery you're suspected of stealing from to speak with the manager might not be a good look if the police find out about it."

"Why not?" They already thought I'd done it anyway. Surely I couldn't make the situation worse.

"They might think you're revisiting the scene of the crime or trying to sway the manager into believing your side of the story."

I pulled a face. He could be right about that, although I wouldn't admit it. Still, when the options were to either be a sitting duck or try to figure out what was going on, the latter would win every time. I couldn't just wait for the police to decide they had enough to make the charges stick.

"Let's do it." I stood up. "If she vouches for me, it could help."

Zeke muttered something under his breath but I couldn't make out the words. I got the gist of it though. He thought I was making the wrong decision.

"If we go and it doesn't work out, then at least we know we tried." I crinkled my nose. I wasn't used to trying to persuade Zeke of anything. Usually it was the other way around, and I didn't know what to make of the change. "Your staff can look into Bergen more while we're gone."

"Fine." He stood and shoved his hands in his pockets. "But just so you know, I think this will backfire."

"I hear you." I raised my chin. "I choose to take the risk."

"Okay." He shrugged. "That's on you then."

I waited while he gave his team instructions, then we took one of the company's black SUVs to the Windy City Gallery. It was a large building, designed in the mid-2000s by a world-renowned architect, with a reflective dome-shaped roof and steel beams forming veins across the surface. A lot of people thought the gallery was beautiful. Personally, I found its exterior cold and soulless, but the interior was divine. High ceilings rose overhead as we entered. The floors were pale wood and the walls were stark white, the better to direct viewers' attention to the artwork.

I headed for the small booth near the entrance. In the morning, there would have been a line of customers, but now, it was much quieter.

"Hi." I smiled at the woman behind the glass. "I'm looking for Patience Heath."

The woman smiled back. "Is she expecting you?"

"No," I admitted. "But we won't take up much of her time."

The woman hesitated. "I can call and see if she's willing to meet with you. Who may I say is looking for her?"

"Fiona Ryan." I searched her eyes for a hint of recognition but thankfully there was nothing. Perhaps the police hadn't shared their suspicions with the gallery yet, or perhaps Patience hadn't shared with the staff.

"One minute, Miss Ryan." She withdrew her cell phone and made a call. I turned away and tried not to eavesdrop as she spoke to Patience. After a few moments, she lowered the phone. "Patience will be here in a minute."

"Thank you very much."

I backed away from the booth, stopping when I sensed a presence behind me.

"Are you sure about this?" Zeke asked, his lips so close to my ear that I shivered.

"Yes." As sure as I could be of anything in my current state.

We waited together in silence until the tapping of heels on the hardwood floor told me somebody was coming. Patience entered the foyer. Her eyebrows knitted together as her gaze fell on me.

"Fiona," she said as she came nearer. "What a surprise to see you here."

"I heard you've had some problems," I said.

"Erm, yes." She pursed her lips. "That's one way to put it."

I reached for her hand, but she stepped back, her eyes widening as if the move shocked her as much as it had me. "I hope you know I didn't do it."

Patience looked uncomfortable. "If anyone has suggested that, it wasn't me."

I rubbed my jaw, frustrated. I wasn't trying to say she had. I just wanted her to see the truth, and I'd been sure she would, but now I felt a hint of doubt. The way she side-eyed Zeke made me wonder if she thought I'd come here to intimidate her, and that he was my muscle.

"I didn't steal those paintings four years ago, and I haven't stolen anything now," I said firmly. "That said, it probably was my fault the theft at the Black Swan Gallery happened. I believe my boyfriend, Bergen, was behind it and used my key card to get access to the gallery."

She frowned. "Did the police look into that?"

"Yes." I sighed. "They didn't agree with me."

"Oh." She glanced at the door she'd come through, as though wondering whether she could make a swift retreat.

"I swear, Patience, I didn't take the Monet. Even if I was a thief, I'd never do that to you. I'm sure it's put your job in jeopardy to have lost such an important piece."

Her eyes flashed. "I didn't lose it. It was stolen."

"But not by me. Don't worry; I'll find out who's behind it." I gestured to Zeke. "This is Zeke Watts, one of the directors of King's Security, which is where I work now. He's going to help me get to the bottom of this."

Patience backed up a step. "I think you should leave that to the police."

"We—" I cut off when Zeke laid a hand on my shoulder. I jerked in surprise. I hadn't expected him to touch me.

"We're just assisting the police as much as we can," Zeke

said with the kind of easy smile he turned on every unsuspecting woman. "The more we can do to help them, the better, right?"

Patience melted in the face of his charm, the stiffness fading from her posture. "I suppose so."

"You're the manager of this gallery?" he asked. I wanted to demand to know where he was going with this line of questioning. I'd already told him she was. But I kept my mouth shut because my approach wasn't getting anywhere and much as I disliked the way he charmed everyone around him, it might be what we needed.

———

ZEKE

I IGNORED THE INDIGNANT REDHEAD AT MY SIDE AND FOCUSED on the pretty brunette we'd come here to talk to.

"Yes, I am," Patience said. "For five years now."

"That's a challenging role. You must have started young." I'd guess she was around the same age as me, so she'd have been in her early thirties when she became manager.

She smiled slightly. "I've worked at art galleries my whole life. My mother was an artist and I inherited her love of art but unfortunately not her aptitude for it."

"I'm sure you're better than you think." Women like her often were. They were simply too critical of themselves to believe it. Fiona was the same way.

She laughed. "I'm really not, but thank you." Her smile warmed a few degrees. "Are you interested in art yourself?"

"I appreciate it, but I can't say I always understand it. I'm definitely not an artist personally. I don't have an artistic bone in my body."

Beside me, Fiona made a sound of disagreement. I nudged her with my elbow, indicating for her to be quiet. I was trying to build a rapport, and I hadn't lied. I wasn't artistic. I just had plenty of creativity in other ways.

"We don't want to put you in a bad position," I said, lowering my voice. "But is there anything you can tell us about the theft that might help us figure out who's behind it?"

She shrugged. "You probably already know the basics. We were supposed to have an exhibition opening last night. My assistant, Glen, was checking the layout a couple of hours before opening when he noticed that something was wrong with the Monet. He called me, and I called the police. They sent a team down and took the forgery away for examination."

Fiona's quiet intake of breath made me think she'd picked up on the same thing I had. Patience's assistant had noticed something wrong with the Monet, not that the Monet was missing. Combined with what I knew of the Black Swan Gallery theft, it sounded as though the Monet had been swapped for a forgery. That meant there was no way to know for sure exactly when it had happened.

"Had the Monet been at the gallery for long?" I asked, hoping to get a time frame for the crime without letting on what I was doing.

"It arrived on Tuesday." Patience rubbed her temples. "It was the real deal. I'd know a legitimate Monet anywhere."

So, someone must have made the exchange sometime between the delivery on Tuesday and Thursday afternoon. I wondered if the delivery company would have a record of what time they'd dropped it off.

"Where was it displayed?" I asked, glad Fiona had remained silent.

"In the special exhibit gallery." She glanced around the mostly empty foyer. "Would you like to see?"

"That would be incredible."

Patience's eyes flicked to Fiona. "You'll have to stay here. Sorry, Fi. You understand."

"I do." Fiona's tone was light, but I could sense her growing frustration. She'd thought Patience would be on her side and, instead, she was being treated like a suspect. I could see where Patience was coming from though. It wouldn't be good optics to allow an alleged thief into the gallery so soon after a theft had occurred—especially when that person was the police's main suspect.

Patience gestured for me to follow her. She led me up a flight of wide marble stairs and turned left. The special exhibition gallery was the second room on the right side of the corridor. She glided in, her heels clacking on the wooden floor, and gestured to the empty wall at the end of the room. A plaque affixed to the wall presumably contained information about *Daisies*, but there was no other sign the painting had ever been there. I scanned the other walls. A series of paintings lined them, most of them flowers or floral arrangements, done in the impressionist style.

A hand curled around my arm and I looked over to find Patience looking up at me.

"It's not a tiny painting," I said. "It's amazing anyone could get it out past security."

Her fingers curled tighter. I hid a grimace. I wanted to dislodge her, but if I did, she might stop cooperating.

"We don't have actual security guards." She sounded embarrassed. "With the security system we have in place, we didn't think we'd need them."

"Even for a painting by an artist as famous as Monet?"

She winced. "It's an oversight that won't happen again."

I felt a pang of sympathy. As Fiona had said, if the

gallery owner decided Patience hadn't done enough to protect the painting, she could lose her job. Hopefully we could resolve matters quickly and it would work out for everyone.

"Who designed your security system?" I asked.

Her lips curled in a wry smile. "King's Security."

"Ah." The back of my neck prickled. I had no doubt she was telling the truth, and it would be easy to verify. The problem was, one of our systems should absolutely have sounded an alarm if someone had walked in here and tried to abscond with a painting that was too big to fit within a backpack or under someone's shirt. I'd designed the tech for our electronic systems myself, and they were virtually unhackable, which meant that either the system had been turned off at the time of the theft or someone had tampered with it. Perhaps an inside person had been involved.

"How many are on the staff here?"

She tilted her head in thought, her dark hair cascading over her shoulders. "Five full-time staff at the gallery itself. There are a few part-timers too. Then there are another handful who work at the café on the ground floor."

That wasn't too many. If we'd installed their system, we probably kept a list of their staff too, so we could cross-check anyone behaving suspiciously on the video feeds against their employee register. I could easily dig through a dozen or so backgrounds to see if any of them looked shady.

I paced the perimeter of the room, taking in every detail. Patience walked at my side, although she'd fortunately had to let go of my arm to avoid making things awkward.

"Thank you for showing me around," I said as we completed the circuit. "I appreciate you being so willing to help."

She gave me a little smile and withdrew a business card

from her pocket. She tucked it into my jacket. "Take this in case you have any questions."

"I'll be in touch." I moved toward the exit and she kept pace with me.

"I hope you will," she said as we reached the top of the stairs.

I flashed a parting smile and hurried down. When I reached the bottom, Fiona glanced at the corner of the card protruding from my pocket.

"Super professional," she snarked.

I placed my hand on the small of her back and guided her out. She could sass me all she liked. I'd gotten more useful information from her so-called old friend than she had.

5

FIONA

I FELT LIKE THROWING SOMETHING AND I HAD NO IDEA WHY. Surely it couldn't have been because of Zeke's flirting with Patience. Why should I care what he did? Except that he'd promised to take this seriously and it didn't feel like he was.

"Did you learn anything interesting other than Patience's phone number?" I asked as we reached the SUV, wincing at the catty note in my voice.

"Actually, yes." He pushed the button to unlock the car and got into the driver's seat.

I yanked the passenger door open and dropped onto the seat. "So?"

He turned to face me, his expression amused. "Calm down, Fifi. I said I'd help you, and I will." He relocked the doors and started the engine. "I think we both guessed that it's likely the Monet was replaced with a forgery, similar to what happened in the Black Swan case four years ago."

I nodded. "I picked up on that too."

He drummed his tattooed fingers against the steering

wheel. "Well, did you know that the Windy City Gallery has one of our security systems installed, or that there are no in-person security guards present?"

"No," I admitted, the heat of frustration inside me cooling down.

"What about the fact that they have five full-time staff, a few part-timers, and others who work in the attached café—most of whom presumably have access to the building?"

I looked down at my lap. Okay, so he'd gotten useful information from Patience. Shame welled within me. I'd had no right to get snarky with him. He was trying to help me, and he had no reason to do that other than being a generally good person. I should know better than to treat him poorly.

"Thank you," I said. "I'm sorry for snapping at you. You didn't deserve that."

"Apology accepted." He pulled out of the park and maneuvered onto the road.

"I don't know why I'm being so rude. It's been a rough day, but that's no excuse. I'll try not to do it again."

He reached over and put his hand on one of mine. "You're allowed to have off days. I know better than to take it personally."

The shame churned in my gut. Of course he'd choose today to be understanding. I felt like even more of a bitch. But then he glanced over, a smirk tugging at the corner of his mouth.

"Besides," he added. "I've had plenty of practice at being rejected by you before."

I huffed and removed his hand from mine. There was the Zeke I knew.

"What should we do now?" I asked, to change the subject.

"You need to go home and take care of yourself," he said.

"Like you said, it's been a rough day. You deserve a little recovery time."

"I can't," I replied automatically. "I mean, I don't want to."

My apartment was as empty as the rest of my personal life. For the past four years, I'd thrown myself into my job with King's Security. I rarely dated. After Bergen's betrayal, it was too difficult to open myself up to anyone again. I worked, did my socializing at the gym, and other than that, my life was depressingly barren.

"Just because you don't want to doesn't mean you shouldn't," he pointed out.

I looked out the side window and pulled a face. He was right, but I really didn't think being alone, in my stark apartment, would help anything. "If you were in my situation—accused of a crime you didn't commit—would you just go home and take a nap?"

I turned to face him just in time to see his jaw clench. Interesting. Usually, he wasn't one to show his emotions about anything.

"No," he admitted. "I'd work my ass off to find out who was responsible and I'd make them pay."

I shivered at the dark promise in his voice. Despite the rumors about his black ops background, I'd never been scared of Zeke. I'd thought of him as mostly harmless. Now, I realized what a mistake that might have been. He sounded like a man who meant what he said.

"I'll take you back to the office," he said after a minute passed in silence.

"Thanks."

We didn't speak for the rest of the journey. My mind was whirring, the events of the day replaying themselves on fast-forward. I wondered if Zeke had ever had cause to get revenge on someone before. I would like the chance to do the same to Bergen. An image of him popped into my head and I wondered where he was. I hadn't been able to figure out where he went when he left me, although I assumed it was somewhere within Chicago since the police said they'd been at his place. I'd have hired a private detective, but my finances had been wiped out. It had taken me years to pay off the debt he'd accrued in my name and by then, there hadn't seemed much point in hunting him down.

When we arrived at the building that housed King's Security, Zeke parked in the underground parking lot and we took the stairs up.

"Are you hungry?" I asked, my stomach growling.

He patted his flat belly. "I could eat."

"I'll stop at the café and get us something."

We parted ways, and I made a beeline to the café. While I stood in line, I looked around, wondering whether any gossip had spread yet about the police having been in to question me. Nobody was staring, but I thought I noticed a couple of pairs of eyes skirt away.

When I reached the counter, I ordered a pasta salad and a caramel latte for me and a sandwich with black coffee for Zeke. I'd ordered lunch for him before when he and Ronan were in meetings together, so I knew what he liked. They called my order, and I carried the food up another flight of stairs and down a corridor, past the open-plan area where Zeke's staff worked, and to his door. Several people smiled at me. I tried to smile back, but it was strained.

I paused in the doorway, watching Zeke read something on his computer screen. His dark hair fell over his forehead and the swirl of a tattoo peeked out from beneath the neckline of his shirt. His expression was intense, and his fingers moved quickly over the keyboard as he began to type. My breath caught, and I tried to tamp down the flutter of attraction low in my gut.

He really was a sexy man. Sexier than Bergen. There was just something about him that was nearly impossible to resist. I pressed my lips together. Had I judged him unfairly because he had a surface resemblance to my ex? I'd never thought so, but after today, I was beginning to believe I might have been wrong about him. Maybe there was more to him than I'd believed.

ZEKE

I sensed Fiona watching me and bit back my instinctive need to ask whether she liked what she saw. I was trying to put her needs first, and that meant less flirting.

"That smells great," I said, turning to face her. "What did you get?"

A flush stained her cheeks, as if she knew that I knew she'd been staring at me. "A chicken sandwich with coffee for you, and pasta salad for me."

"Thanks, Fi."

See? I didn't even call her "Fifi."

She set my coffee and meal on my desk, then took hers to the chair she'd brought in earlier and sipped her drink. Whatever it was, it smelled sweet.

"Need a sugar high as well as a caffeine pick-me-up?" I asked.

"Whatever will keep me going."

I considered pointing out that she didn't have to keep going. She could leave the research to me and my team while she took a much-needed nap, but I understood why she didn't want to. She no doubt felt powerless, and being involved would help her feel like she was doing something.

"I've pulled up the gallery's staff list," I told her, grabbing the sandwich and pulling it closer. "It seems the cafe staff don't have access to the gallery itself outside of normal working hours. Their key cards allow them to enter the building via a side door, but provided the doors between the cafe and the gallery are locked overnight, they can't get further in. It's up to whomever opens the gallery to unlock the connecting door." I bit into my sandwich and moaned. She'd remembered exactly how I liked it. I shouldn't be surprised. Fiona was one of the most competent people I knew.

"What about the part-timers you mentioned?" she asked. "Do they have key cards?"

I chewed and swallowed. "Not according to our records."

"So that leaves the gallery staff," she mused, digging her fork into a piece of pasta.

"And three of the artists whose work they display." I hadn't thought to ask about that earlier, but fortunately, whoever installed their system had kept good records.

"Interesting." She looked thoughtful. "That's not common. Or at least, it didn't used to be."

"Worth looking into?" I asked around another mouthful of food.

"Isn't everything?"

"At this point, yes." If we got new information to narrow things down, we could be more selective about who or what we investigated, but for now, there were no bad leads.

I finished the sandwich and washed it down with coffee, then wiped my fingers on a napkin and returned them to the keyboard. "The criminal records for each staff member are in this file too. Let's check them, shall we?" I opened Patience's first. As I'd expected, she was squeaky clean. "Not even a parking ticket for your buddy Patience."

Next, I checked her assistant, Glen. Unlike Patience, he

did have a couple of parking tickets, and one for speeding, but other than that, there was nothing of interest. One by one, I opened the others and scanned the summaries. Clean. Clean. Another speeding ticket.

"No red flags?" Fiona asked.

"Nope." The first of the three artists with a key card was a different story. "Here we go." I sat up straighter. "One arrest for drunk and disorderly behavior, another for assault during a bar fight, and a D.U.I." I checked the photograph. The guy was in his late forties or early fifties with gray facial hair and deep-set eyes. "Andrew Garnet. Heard of him?"

"He paints abstracts," she said. "Mostly in shades of red and black. He's talented, but there's something disturbing about his work. I wouldn't like to be inside his mind."

I noted his name on a piece of paper. He might be worth questioning, although being a violent drunk was a far cry from stealing a priceless painting. I opened the next artist's background check.

"Huh. This guy was charged with possession of a controlled substance and intent to distribute." I found his name. "Sam Robbins. Ring any bells?"

She shook her head. "No, sorry."

I looked at Sam's headshot. He was younger, perhaps in his late twenties, and his cheekbones were hollow, his face gaunt.

"I thought artists were goody-two-shoes," I said. "You know, all classy and highbrow. Isn't that how art is portrayed?"

Fiona laughed, and my heart lifted at the sound. She'd been too withdrawn today. "Most of them aren't squeaky clean. I'm sure some are, but for many, their angst fuels their work. They draw inspiration from everything they've been through."

I frowned, noticing that she'd referred to artists as

"them" and "they." I'd been under the impression she was something of an artist herself, but the way she was speaking didn't support that theory.

"Aren't you an artist?" I asked.

She waved her hand dismissively. "Not like these guys. So, who's the last one?"

I glanced at the final name. "Sandra Michaels." I raised an eyebrow. "She's clean as a whistle."

Sandra Michaels appeared to be an older woman who'd behaved herself for her whole life.

"So, what next?" Fiona asked.

I drummed my fingers on the desk. "We talk to the staff in person. Unless you have a better idea?"

"Unfortunately not."

I nodded. "We'll start with Sam and Andrew since they might have substance abuse problems, which can cause people to make poor decisions, then move on to the others. We can't do that tonight though."

"Why not?" she demanded.

"It's too late for us to reach out. We're not the police. People aren't obligated to talk to us, so if we barge in there at this time of night, they're unlikely to tell us anything."

She grimaced. "I guess that's a fair point."

I grinned. "Can I get that in writing? 'Zeke was right.'"

"No." Her lips pressed together. "You'll never hear it again."

"Ah well, worth a shot."

She rolled her eyes. "What about Bergen? Shouldn't we be looking into him?"

I crossed my arms. "Do you know where he lives?"

"No," she admitted.

"I'll see if I can find him in the DMV register and we can go from there. Again, even if we get his address, turning up now won't do us any favors. We need to be more strategic."

I could see that she wanted to argue, but she kept her mouth shut. Technically, I shouldn't have access to the DMV records, but I didn't let that stop me. I ran a search and found our guy. Fiona leaned forward and I quickly minimized out of the tab, afraid that if she saw his address, she'd take it upon herself to pay him a visit. I searched for, and wrote down, addresses for the other people we wanted to check out, and by the time Fiona and I had made our action list for tomorrow, the office outside was dim and everyone had left.

"Let me take you home," I said. She'd already missed the train she usually took. Not that I was a stalker who knew her schedule.

"But..." She trailed off.

"Come on." I stood and held out a hand. She took it and pulled herself up, then cleared away the trash from our food. We headed down to the basement level, where I escorted her to my car.

She stopped and raised an eyebrow at the mid-range silver hatchback. "I expected you to drive something flashier."

"Nah. This baby is better for tailing people or going unnoticed." I patted the hood. "No one expects a mom car to be following them."

I'd never fully believe that no one was watching me. With the circumstances under which I'd left the agency, I was sure they kept me under surveillance. Fortunately, Fiona didn't ask any follow-up questions. She got in and directed me to her apartment. We were quiet as we drove, and I couldn't help wondering what was going on in her head. I didn't ask though, and soon, I parked outside her building. She hesitated and glanced at me.

"Would you like to come up for a coffee?" She raised her

finger. "I really mean coffee. This isn't an invitation to get me into bed."

I studied her face. I'd expected her to be glad to be rid of me, but she looked reluctant to leave. Perhaps she didn't want to be alone.

"Sure."

I followed her to her apartment on the third floor, curious to see the inside. When she unlocked the door and pushed it open, I was surprised by the sight that greeted us. The apartment was nearly bare. The walls were unadorned and almost as starkly white as the interior of the gallery had been. The carpet was threadbare and while I could see a sofa and two armchairs, there were no cozy touches like throws or cushions, which I'd expected from her.

I frowned. This didn't feel like a place where Fiona should live. It reminded me of my own condo, which I'd intentionally kept minimalistic. Fiona should be surrounded by color. She was vibrant, and her home should be the same way. Not like this.

6

———

FIONA

I WOKE WITH A START AS SOMETHING CLATTERED IN THE kitchen. I jolted upright, clasping the blanket to my chest. The light of dawn filtered through the curtains. I heard another muffled noise and eased out of bed, my pulse racing. Someone was in my apartment. No one other than the super had a key, so who the hell was it and how had they gotten in? I'd definitely locked the door after Zeke left last night. I was sure of that because I'd checked it several times before going to bed.

I tiptoed across the room, looking for something I could use to defend myself. A baseball bat would come in handy right now, but I didn't have anything like that. I didn't even have anything in approximately that shape. I scanned my dresser and shelves, my eyes settling on a pair of heavy stiletto pumps. I grabbed one of them and held it up like a hammer, ready to brain whoever had broken in.

My fingers curled around the edge of the door and eased it open. The bottom whispered over the carpet but I didn't

49

think it had made enough noise for anyone to notice. I padded out, my bare feet silent on the floor. As I edged into the living room, I heard a murmured voice. People talking? Or just one person? I peeked into the kitchen and my shoulders slumped.

"For fuck's sake, Zeke. You scared the crap out of me. What are you doing here?"

Zeke looked up from where he was setting up drip coffee on the kitchen counter. He tossed his shaggy hair out of his eyes and grinned. "I'm making breakfast. What does it look like I'm doing?" His gaze flew to the shoe. "Death by pump. Very Agatha Christie. Would you mind putting it down now that you know I'm not an intruder?"

"Still an intruder," I muttered under my breath. "What time is it?"

"A little after seven."

"Jesus." I dragged my hand down my face. "And you're here...why?"

He slid a paper bag I hadn't noticed across the counter. "I knew you'd want to get an early start on our next steps." He paused and looked me up and down. "Or was I wrong about that? Because if you'd rather spend the morning in bed..."

I groaned, the back of my neck heating as I realized that I was wearing a thin silk slip that barely brushed the tops of my thighs and made it perfectly clear I didn't have a bra on underneath. I tucked my arms across my chest to hide my nipples, which were always perky in the morning. It had nothing to do with Zeke, no matter what the smug bastard might think.

I backed up, retreating toward the bedroom. "How did you get in here?"

He leaned one elbow on the counter and smiled lopsidedly. "King's Security keeps spare keys for all of its staff members in case of emergency, or did you forget that?"

"This isn't an emergency."

He shrugged. "That's your opinion. Why don't you join me for breakfast? The coffee will be done soon and I have a berry Danish that's calling your name."

My lips parted in shock. "How did you know they're my favorite?"

He touched the side of his nose. "A man has to keep his secrets."

Nosy bastard. Yet something warm unfurled inside my chest at the thought that he'd paid attention to what I liked and gone out of his way to get it. While intrusive, there was something sweet about that.

"I'll grab my robe and be out in a minute," I said.

"Don't feel like you have to," he called after me.

I rolled my eyes as I unhooked my warmest robe from behind the door and slipped it on. No doubt he wouldn't mind eating breakfast with me half-naked, but I didn't intend to give him a show. I pulled on a pair of socks, drew in a steadying breath, and returned to the kitchen. He was now sitting on a stool by the breakfast bar, a coffee in front of him and a filled pastry of some variety on a plate in front of him. He'd dished up the berry Danish and another coffee for me.

"I added caramel syrup and a little milk," he said as I pulled out the stool beside his. "I get the impression you aren't a black coffee kind of girl."

"I'm not, thanks." I didn't know what to make of his thoughtfulness. I'd always considered Zeke to be self-centered, but he'd been proving me wrong with every inter-action over the past two days. That sense of shame bubbled up again. I had judged him more harshly than he deserved. I'd have to do better from now on.

I cut into my Danish and closed my eyes as I popped it into my mouth, the sweet tartness of the berries exploding on my tongue. When I opened my eyes, I found Zeke staring at me, his eyes fastened on my mouth.

I flushed, and my stomach flipped over. "Sorry, I really love these things."

"Don't be sorry." He spoke in a rasp. "It's sexy as fuck."

My face flamed and I took another bite, trying really hard not to look like my taste buds were orgasming. "Are we starting with Bergen this morning?"

He nodded. "I thought we'd drop by the address listed on his DMV record. If we learn anything interesting from him, we can follow that up, or alternatively, we can move on to the artists with the criminal histories."

"Sounds good." Although my stomach churned at the thought of seeing Bergen again. I hadn't seen him since the morning I'd woken in his arms, made us breakfast, and gone to work, clueless to the fact that he'd be gone by the time I returned and my life would be in tatters. "We should check in with Ronan too."

He winked. "Already done."

At another time, I might have been annoyed by his high-handedness about something that affected me more than him, but I didn't have the energy for that. I was just glad he was helping.

"Great." I sipped the coffee. It was surprisingly good. "I'll finish this and then shower. We can go afterward."

Zeke waggled his eyebrows. "Want any company?" Before I could reply, his face fell. "Sorry, I'm not supposed to be doing that."

"Doing what? Joining me for a shower?"

He shook his head. "Don't worry about it. Go shower. I'll be here when you get out."

ZEKE

ONCE I HEARD THE SHOWER START, I COUNTED OUT THREE minutes and made my way as quietly as possible to Fiona's bedroom. As I opened the door, a wave of her scent drifted out, deliciously floral. Tempting and sultry, just like the woman herself.

The room was depressingly similar to the rest of the apartment. White walls, bland furniture, and no photos or art. The only splash of color was the blue and purple bedspread. I withdrew a bug scanner from my pocket and walked around the room. I waved it over the furniture and paused at the nightstand, taking care to run it past each drawer. I'd checked the rest of the apartment last night, after she went to bed, but I hadn't wanted to risk waking her up by sneaking into the bedroom.

When I was satisfied there were no listening devices present, I slipped out again, closing the door behind me, and returned to my seat at the breakfast bar. I wasn't sure who was more likely to have bugged the apartment—the police or whoever had set her up—but I'd thought it reasonable to assume that both parties would want to keep a close eye on her. Fortunately, she seemed to be in the clear, although I wanted to run a check on her cell phone too. It was issued by King's Security, with our anti-hacking software installed, so there was probably nothing to worry about, but it was better to be safe than sorry.

I drank more coffee, enjoying the pleasant zip of caffeine entering my body. The shower shut off and I cleaned away the breakfast dishes, trying to ignore the noises coming from the other room. I couldn't afford to think of Fiona undressed and glistening wet. My body tightened and I cursed.

Get a hold of yourself.

Just because I'd wanted to see her, touch her, and taste her for years didn't mean I couldn't control myself around her.

"Hey," she said as she emerged into the living area. I gulped. I was used to seeing her in office attire, which meant form-fitting dresses with respectably high necklines and long skirts. This morning, however, she'd opted to wear a pair of navy jeans that hugged her slender thighs and a floaty green blouse that made her look soft and touchable.

I forced myself to get it together. "Ready to go?"

She clutched a cream-colored leather purse in one hand and had a black jacket slung over her shoulder. "Yes. Let's do it."

The cab of my car felt smaller today than it had yesterday. Fiona's floral scent was stronger—she must have used perfume or a scented lotion after getting out of the shower —and it wrapped around me and made my cock take notice.

I glanced at her out of the corner of my eye as I followed GPS directions to Bergen Cole's last known address. I couldn't help wondering what might be different between us if she hadn't been burned by her asshole ex. She might have agreed to go out with me when we'd first met. If that had happened, we could have been living together by now, in which case I'd have been able to give her an alibi for the theft of the Monet.

But then, there was always the chance that if she'd gone out with me, we'd have slept together and nothing more would have come of it. I might not have appreciated her strength and wit the way I do now. It was crappy to admit, but the fact she'd shut me down had gone a long way toward hooking my attention. I hated to think what I could have missed out on if I'd had her and taken her for granted.

"You're quiet," she said as we stopped at a traffic light.

"Just thinking."

I readied myself for her to make a smart-ass remark about how unlike me that was, but it never came. I snuck a look at her. Was she all right?

When we arrived, it wasn't difficult to see that Bergen Cole's apartment building was nicer than Fiona's. It still wasn't much to look at though. I stayed close to her as we took the stairs to his floor and strode along the corridor, counting the door numbers. When we reached the number listed by the DMV, I paused.

"Are you sure you're ready for this?" I asked.

She bit her lip, visibly hesitant, but then nodded. "Just do it."

I knocked before she had a chance to second-guess herself. A distant grunt came from somewhere within, and then I could hear sounds as someone moved closer. I felt Fiona stiffen beside me as the door handle turned and swung inward.

"Hello?" An older gentleman with red-rimmed eyes and a New Jersey accent blinked sleepily out at us. He was definitely not Bergen Cole. "What kind of time do you call this?"

I glanced at my watch. "Eight forty-five."

"Exactly." His beady eyes narrowed. "On a Saturday." He huffed. "What are you selling, anyway?"

"We're not selling anything." Fiona stepped forward and smiled at him. "We're looking for Bergen Cole. He lives here. I'm an old friend of his and I thought I'd surprise him while we're in town."

"Bergen Cole?" The old guy looked confused. "Ain't no one here by that name. I'm Merv. This has been my place for going on eighteen months now."

"Does anyone live with you?" I asked.

He scowled. "What? Gonna rub it in that I'm all on my lonesome? No, asshole. No one lives with me."

Fiona's friendly expression didn't waver. "Do you know who had the apartment before you?"

Merv shrugged. "I heard it was some artist guy who moved to Seattle. Don't know his name."

Fiona and I exchanged a look.

"Thank you," she said. "We're sorry to have bothered you. Have a lovely day."

Grumbling, Merv shut the door in our faces.

I ran a hand through my hair. "I guess he's not here then."

"Are you sure it was this apartment?" she asked. "You didn't get the number wrong?"

"I'm certain." I didn't make mistakes like that. In my previous line of work, they could have been deadly. Unfortunately, Bergen's absence raised an issue I'd rather not broach. "We may have to consider the fact that your ex isn't the one behind the theft."

Fiona gasped. Her mouth dropped open and she glared at me like she wanted to slap me. I inwardly sighed. I hadn't missed that look.

"I'm not saying he isn't," I clarified. "But we need to keep an open mind."

7

FIONA

"Who else could it possibly be?" I demanded, glancing along the corridor to make sure no one could overhear us. "The painting was replaced with a forgery. The similarities were enough for the police to think it was me. It must be him."

Bergen was a devious toad. He'd manipulated me, stolen from me, and let me down in every conceivable way. He had to be responsible for my current problems. He'd used me as a patsy once, so it made sense he'd do it again.

"Let's just look at this as if we're impartial observers," Zeke said, holding up his hands in a calming gesture. As if that really calmed anyone. "You can't be one hundred percent certain he stole those paintings from the Black Swan Gallery four years ago. Sure, the fact he disappeared out of your life that day looks guilty, but you don't have irrefutable proof."

I folded my arms over my chest defensively but I couldn't contradict him.

"On the slight chance he didn't do it, then someone else could be behind both crimes," he said. "We should look for other connections between them."

"You mean like someone who worked at both places?"

"Yes, or someone else who had access. An artist, contractor, even the janitor."

I nodded briskly and stalked down the corridor toward the stairs. Logically, I could see that his idea had merit, but I couldn't help feeling like he was just another person who didn't believe me. Emotion thickened the back of my throat and I was glad Zeke had stopped trying to talk to me for a few seconds because if I had to speak, he'd no doubt hear how upset I was, and I didn't like being vulnerable with him. Honestly, I wasn't sure that Zeke was the kind of person anyone ever wanted to be vulnerable with.

Once I'd managed to get my breathing under control, I slowed until we were walking together.

"I hear you," I said. "I'm willing to look into other possibilities, but I still think Bergen did it and whether or not you agree, I'm not going to stop trying to chase him down."

To my surprise, he smiled. "I didn't expect anything else. I just don't want you to have blinders on when it comes to him."

"I'll try not to." I started down the stairs, taking them quickly and enjoying the faint burn in my legs. I was grateful he hadn't completely dismissed my concerns about Bergen, although I did feel a bit called out by the fact he obviously thought I was obsessed with Bergen's guilt. Yes, I had a one-track mind, but if Zeke had been through what I had—the hours of interrogation, the way nobody I knew trusted me anymore, and having to dig myself out of a financial hole I hadn't caused—he'd feel the same way.

"Why don't we start with Andrew?" he suggested as we reached the ground floor.

"Actually..." I bit my lip, silently weighing our options. "I have another idea."

"What's that?"

"Yesterday, while I was waiting for you and Patience to finish doing whatever you were doing, I noticed a painting by an acquaintance of mine on the gallery wall. He also sold artwork through the Black Swan Gallery, so if you're looking for connections, he might be a good place to start."

I didn't think for a second that Denny had anything to do with the thefts, but he was a gossip, so he might have useful information. He was also a friendly face—one of only few of my old colleagues who had stood by me—and I could really do with one of his hugs right about now.

Zeke shrugged. "If you think it's worthwhile. Do you know where we can find this acquaintance of yours?"

"I do." I gave him the address and climbed into his car. I could still hardly believe he drove a hatchback. I'd been sure he was a sports car guy.

He drove us to Denny's home in a trendy upscale neighborhood. He was only able to afford the house because he shared it with several other artists. They claimed being so near to the park helped fill their creative wells. I'd never had the same affinity for nature, but they all did beautiful work, so there was no arguing with their process.

"It's this one." I pointed to the building and Zeke parked on the roadside opposite. I got out of the car and waited for him to join me. Together, we crossed the road and climbed three stairs to the door. I knocked and stepped back.

A moment later, the door flew open and Denny beamed out at me.

"Fiona!" He wrapped his arms around me and hugged me tight. I buried my face in his shoulder, soaking up the human contact. I got far too little of it. "It's so good to see you, darling. What brings you here?"

ZEKE

MY EYES NARROWED AT THE FAMILIAR WAY THE MAN IN THE hipster glasses held onto Fiona. I hadn't been prepared for his reaction to her, and I didn't like being caught off guard. She hadn't mentioned being friends with this guy—just acquaintances—and it made me wonder what else she might not have mentioned. My gaze lingered on his hand where it rested on her mid-back. At least it hadn't sank any lower. If he'd touched her too intimately, I might have had to remove his hand from her body, and I doubt either of them would like my methods.

I took the opportunity to assess him while he was preoccupied with my beautiful partner. He was a little taller than Fiona, but shorter than me. Slender but athletic, with tidy facial hair and vivid blue eyes. He was good-looking, if you liked the cute nerd type. Based on the fact Fiona had dated Bergen, I had assumed she preferred her men tattooed and rugged, but maybe she didn't have a type at all. It wasn't as if I had a physical type. I liked all women—the more fiery, the better.

"We have something to talk to you about," Fiona said in answer to the guy's question. She looked around. "In private."

"Oh, sure." He sounded intrigued. "Come in. Can I get you a coffee? I remember how much you love your skinny caramel lattes."

"Maybe just a little one." She flashed him a smile. "I've already had one coffee this morning."

He beamed. "One latte, heavy on the caramel, light on

the coffee, coming right up." He turned to me and his eyes widened. He scanned me up and down, blatant appreciation in his eyes. "And who do we have here?"

Fiona sighed. "This is Zeke. He's helping me out with a problem I'm having."

"Oh, sweetie." He cringed. "Another problem?"

Fiona's face scrunched. "Yup." She met my eyes. "Zeke, this charmer is Denny. He's a fabulous watercolor artist."

Denny preened. "I try." He moved to the side and waved us in. "It's a pleasure to meet you, Zeke. Can I get you a coffee?"

"No, thanks." I had a strict limit on how much caffeine I consumed each day. Too much made me jittery. I'd prefer to wait until later, when I really needed a boost.

"Suit yourself." Denny closed the door behind us and led us down a hallway to an airy living area that was awash with natural light. Fiona sat on one of four armchairs positioned around a coffee table and crossed her legs. I took another of the seats while Denny fussed with coffee in the attached open-plan kitchen. When he returned, he passed Fiona a mug of frothy milk and placed a small cup of espresso in front of himself.

"So, what's the drama?" he asked.

I glanced at Fiona, wondering how much she'd divulge. While the police hadn't told us to keep quiet about the theft, it hadn't hit the papers yet so I couldn't imagine they'd want it being widely shared.

"Another painting has been stolen," she said. "From the Windy City Gallery. The police think I took it."

I watched Denny's reaction carefully. He rolled his eyes and made a scoffing sound, seeming to immediately dismiss the possibility. Because he trusted her, or because he knew who'd actually done it?

"You haven't had anything to do with art for years," Denny said. "What ridiculous reason could they possibly have to think you were involved?"

"We don't know."

I was impressed by how little her expression gave away. Once again, I couldn't help wondering if Fiona had plenty of practice at lying. Although I supposed it wasn't technically a lie. We may have suspected why the police had come to her, but we didn't know for certain.

"You poor darling. I'm so sorry they're putting you through this." His eyes were soft with sympathy, and his tone sounded genuine. "What can I do to help? Do you need another one of my famous hugs?"

Fiona laughed. "There's no such thing as too many hugs, but actually, I thought we'd come to you since you have art at both the Black Swan Gallery and the Windy City Gallery. I thought if anyone had any idea who might have done something like that, it would be you."

Denny looked pleased, and I sent Fiona an approving look. She clearly knew how to butter the guy up.

"Honestly, Fi, I hate to dwell on thoughts of who might have done something this awful. Not only the crimes but to set you up too." He shook his head. "Despicable."

I hid a grin. He was saying all the right things, but he sounded a little too delighted for his regret to be genuine. I knew the type. He thrived on gossip.

"Who do you think it could have been?" Fiona persisted. "Has Patience had a falling-out with anyone?"

Denny pulled a face. "Patience is so wonderfully tepid that nobody could hate her enough to want to mess with her career. No, it's more likely that someone needed the cash." He rubbed his chin, his expression thoughtful. "Andrew never has enough money, and sweet Sandra has been known to gamble online a bit too much."

My eyebrows flew up. Sandra, the elderly lady with the clean record, was a secret gambler?

"But Sandra wouldn't go into debt, would she?" Fiona asked, as if she knew the woman.

"I wouldn't have thought so," Denny agreed. "But you can never know for sure these days. The skeletons some people hide in their closets. Dear God."

I clasped my hands together on my lap, wondering what he'd think if he could see all the skeletons in *my* closet. There were many. I'd done bad things in my former career. Always for the right reason—or so I was told—but I hadn't been surprised when life gave me a karmic kick up the ass. I'd probably deserved it. Not that that meant I'd ever forgive the people responsible.

"What about Sam?" Fiona asked.

"Hmm. Sam." Denny sipped his coffee. "He's off the hard stuff these days and I don't think he'd risk doing something stupid when he's worked hard to turn things around."

Fiona tasted her latte, then licked her lips. My gut tightened with the longing to taste them.

She raised the mug again. "Have you seen Bergen around at all?"

Denny's eyes lit with mischief. "I wondered when we'd get to him."

She lifted one shoulder and dropped it. "Yeah, well. You know me. I always thought Bergen was the person who'd done it."

"So you did. As a matter of fact, I do think I saw Bergen outside the gallery recently, but it was only for a few seconds, and I couldn't be sure it was him."

Fiona tensed. She turned to me, victory in her eyes. I let her have the moment. For all we knew, Denny was stretching the truth. He seemed like the kind of guy who enjoyed a good story, and being the source of this scandalous tidbit obviously pleased him. We still had to check out other possibilities.

"Where were you two nights ago?" I asked, speaking for the first time since we'd sat down.

Denny's mouth fell open. "I... You..." He sputtered. "I was here, playing video games with three of my roommates. We were here all night. I can wake one of them up if you need to verify, officer."

His snarky tone made me smile. I could see why he and Fiona got along.

"No need for that. And I'm not an officer."

"Oh." He looked intrigued. "I should have known. You don't carry yourself like one. What are you then?"

"He can't tell you that or he'd have to kill you," Fiona teased.

I forced myself to smile even though the comment hit too close to home. There had been a time, when I was deeply embedded in an international cyber terrorist cell, that the words would have been true. Fortunately, that wasn't my life anymore.

"Color me intrigued," Denny said, but he didn't push for more information. He and Fiona chatted for a few more minutes and then she finished her drink and told him we needed to be on our way. He walked us to the door, hugging her again before we left. I bristled at the sight—I didn't like her being held by another man—but I didn't get the impression that either of them was interested in the other, so I let it go.

Once we were in the car again, I turned to her. "Why didn't you tell me you were friends with him?"

She flushed guiltily. "I didn't think it mattered. I knew he'd be helpful, and I thought that was all that was important."

I grunted. "It would have been nice to know."

I'd had enough of being blindsided by people in my life-time, and even though my instincts told me I could trust her, part of me wondered. Part of me would always wonder.

8

———

FIONA

I wasn't sure why Zeke seemed so bothered by our visit with Denny. He usually took everything in stride and it unnerved me to see him thrown off balance. After we left, we dropped by Andrew's place. He was clearly hungover and didn't have much to say for himself, but there was no sign of a Monet in his living room, and honestly, with how much of a mess he was, I doubted he'd have been able to mastermind a heist like that anyway.

While we were with Andrew, Zeke had his staff dig into Sandra. They confirmed that she gambled, but from what they could tell, she wasn't in a financial hole. We dropped by to ask her a few questions, and I felt terrible about how pale she got when Zeke brought up the gambling. It didn't take long before she showed us the door. I got the feeling she wasn't hiding anything though, and Zeke seemed to think the same.

Sam the recovering addict appeared to be living his best life. His eyes were clear, his complexion smooth, and while he clearly hadn't liked us turning up on his doorstep, he'd been patient and polite. We paid a visit to each of the gallery's staff members, although two of them weren't at home—presumably, they were at the gallery—under the guise of checking on the effectiveness of King's Security's system to determine how we could improve it in the future.

By the time we finished, I was mentally and emotionally exhausted. I dealt with people constantly every day. I answered dozens of phone calls and fielded hundreds of emails, but for some reason, doing this had drained me more than dealing with demanding middle management and entitled customers ever had.

"Let's get lunch," Zeke said as we returned to his car after another deflating interview. "You need a break, and I'm hungry."

I was tempted to argue that I could keep going for as long as he could, but he had a point. At this rate, I'd be no use to anyone. "All right."

He looked surprised by my easy acquiescence but didn't comment on it. "What would you like? Italian? Turkish? Indian?"

"How about sushi?" I always found sushi to be a refreshing pick-me-up. Plus it was something I wouldn't have to work off at the gym later in the week. I'd left thirty in the rearview mirror a couple of years ago and staying trim took more effort than it used to.

"Great." He grinned. "I know just the place."

A few minutes later, he pulled up outside Sushi Ya. I side-eyed him. There was no way this was a coincidence. Not after he'd brought the berry Danish this morning.

"You know my favorite sushi place," I said.

He put the car into park, switched off the engine, and unbuckled. "You should assume I know everything, Fifi. I usually do."

"Stalker."

He touched his hand to his heart. "I'm hurt you could think that. I'm just thorough. No stone left unturned."

"I'm counting on it." Perhaps I found his attitude frustrating, but if it got me out of hot water, I wouldn't complain. Besides, despite being unsettled that he seemed to know far more about me than I did about him, I couldn't help being flattered that he'd been interested enough to find these things out about me. Many of the men I'd dated over the years hadn't bothered to learn as much about me as Zeke had, and I'd have willingly told them anything they wanted to know.

He escorted me inside and we removed our shoes at the door and sat on cushions on the floor around a low table. A waiter took our orders and brought us a jug of water. I filled two glasses. My phone buzzed, and I glanced at the screen to see that I had a message from Sage. I opened it.

Sage: *Are you okay? I'm sending you positive energy.*

A smile stole across my face. I adored Sage. She was an absolute sweetheart, and I immediately felt better any time she got in touch with me. I tapped out a reply.

Fiona: *I'm doing as well as I can. Thanks for checking in.*

"Who's that?" Zeke asked.

"Sage," I murmured, slipping the phone into my bag. "Just checking up on me. She's so lovely."

"She is," he agreed. "Too good for Kade, but she doesn't seem to realize it yet."

I rolled my eyes. He and Kade cared for each other, even if they would never admit it. They liked teasing each other far too much. "They're perfect together."

"They're okay." His expression softened. "She's good for him."

"She really is." Kade had always been kind, but he'd also kept himself at an emotional distance for the first few years

I'd known him. It was only now that he was beginning to thaw and let us see more of his real self.

I glanced at Zeke across the table. I still hadn't seen past his emotional barriers, but I appreciated how hard he was working to help me even if he'd never let me in.

"Thank you, if I haven't already said it enough. I appreciate everything you're doing for me."

For a moment, his dark eyes seemed to warm, and I thought he might say something real, but then it was as if a shutter slammed closed.

"All part of the service," he quipped.

Ugh. I rubbed my temple, not wanting to let him see how much it frustrated me when he brushed off the chance for a real connection. For the first time, I wondered why he did it. Was it just the way he was, or had he learned the habit from someone in his past?

I could ask. What would he say if I did? Would he deflect the question like he did everything else, or would I shock him into dropping the act? Because the more time I spent with him, the more I realized that the cavalier attitude I found so jarring wasn't the real him. It was a role he played.

I opened my mouth, ready to ask about his shady past since he knew all about mine, but then I closed it again. Whatever his past was, it was darker than a couple of accusations of theft, and deep down, I wasn't sure I wanted to know.

Coward.

ZEKE

· · ·

Fiona was oddly subdued as we finished our lunch. After the waiter took our plates away, I suggested we return to the office to touch base with Ronan and Kade, who'd both said they'd be in even though it was the weekend.

"Sure," was all she said.

We drove to the office, where she insisted on taking the stairs. I usually did anyway, but it amazed me how someone who never wore a heel less than two inches high could be so eager to walk more than necessary. Of course, I took full advantage of the opportunity to stroll behind her and appreciate her pert ass and sleek legs. She worked hard at them. It would be disrespectful of me not to notice. I didn't say anything though, because I was being a good boy.

As soon as we got there, Willow rushed out of Ronan's office.

"Are you okay?" She opened her arms wide, and Fiona stepped into her embrace. "Ronan told me a little about what's going on. Is there anything you need?"

Fiona didn't seem to know how to respond. For a long moment, she didn't say anything. But then, perhaps having support wasn't something she was used to. Her apartment certainly hadn't given the impression that she had company over much.

"Thank you," she said eventually. "I'm okay. Obviously the situation isn't ideal, but the guys are being amazing about helping me."

"Of course they are." Willow drew back and scanned Fiona's face as if to double-check she really was all right. "You're part of the family."

Fiona's eyes grew suspiciously shiny. I was tempted to tease her about it but I didn't want to ruin the mood.

"Will you tell me more?" Willow asked her. "Ronan wouldn't go into much detail."

"I suppose so." Fiona sounded flustered, but she allowed Willow to take her hand and draw her into a meeting room.

When they were gone, Ronan beckoned me into his office.

"What's up?" I asked as I closed the door behind myself.

"Debrief." Ronan dropped into the chair behind his massive desk. "Give me a rundown on how your interviews went this morning."

I gave him an overview of the people we'd visited and my impressions of them, then waited to hear his thoughts.

"None of them are obvious suspects," he said. "Although it sounds as though at least a couple have the potential to turn to something like theft under the right circumstances. Without knowing more about their personal backgrounds, it's hard to say who might have the contacts necessary to fence a painting like *Daisies.*" He sighed. "It would have been much easier if the janitor had been a wanted con man or if one of the artists were deep in debt."

I smirked. "Nothing is ever that easy."

"True." He leaned back and gazed at me evenly. "Who do you like for it?"

"Honestly?" I shrugged. "I can't be sure yet. It's possible Fiona is right about her ex. Like you said, no one else we've spoken to is an obvious candidate."

"What about the gallery manager herself?" he asked.

"Her record is cleaner than a nun's conscience." I paused to consider the idea more fully. "She would have access to the painting and no one would think anything of her being there out of hours. It's also possible she's come into contact with black market dealers or fences over the course of her career. But it seems unlikely she'd be involved. She's the one whose neck is on the line if the gallery owner decides she didn't do enough to protect the painting."

"Good point." Ronan rubbed his chin in thought. "I was

able to confirm that the painting was replaced by a forgery." He hesitated, then added, "Glen Boomer's key card was used to access the gallery early on Thursday morning. When the police checked, it was in his possession, but he has a rock solid alibi for the time the card was used. He was across town in a spin class with more than twenty witnesses."

"Huh." That was an interesting tidbit. Either someone had swiped the card and returned it to him before he noticed it was gone, or they'd cloned it.

"The police checked and it didn't appear to have been tampered with," Ronan said, as if reading my mind.

"So most likely, someone took it, used it to steal the painting, and put it back without him seeing," I said.

"It sounds far-fetched, doesn't it?" Ronan agreed. "But that's the theory we have to operate from."

"All right then."

"There's something else." The strain in his voice drew my attention.

"What?" I asked.

"I hadn't realized this, but when Fiona was at art school, she specialized in the study of impressionist art and art history. Her final thesis paper was about one of Monet's lesser-known works."

I whistled. "Damn."

In the context, that did sound incriminating. I could understand why the police had immediately thought of her. And shit, this wasn't something we should have been blind-sided by. Fiona should have told us this from the beginning.

"Not a good look," I said. "Not unless the style she favors is 'guilty as hell.'"

9

FIONA

I EXPLAINED THE SITUATION TO WILLOW AND COULDN'T HELP smiling as she said what she'd like to do to Bergen. Willow came across as calm and collected, but she had a hidden fire that had served her well. She was also surprisingly creative in thinking of ways to punish men who deserved it.

"How has it been working with Zeke?" she asked. "I know you and him don't get along very well."

"It's been better than I expected," I admitted. "It annoys me that he's not sold on the idea of Bergen being behind it, but I know it's probably smart to keep an open mind."

"Yeah." Willow grimaced. "I was determined to see Ronan as the enemy when he was looking to take over Lennox Securities, but the more I learned about him, the more I realized I was wrong. Being open-minded isn't easy, but it pays off."

"Let's hope so." Although honestly, I wasn't completely ready to let go of the possibility of nailing Bergen. I stood. "Let's see what those men are up to."

She gave me a quick hug. "We'll get this figured out."

I closed my eyes and allowed myself to enjoy the embrace. I wasn't usually much of a hugger, but today, I needed them from anyone who was willing to give them. We left the meeting room, and Zeke stuck his head out of Ronan's office to wave us in. There weren't enough seats for both of us around the table so I stayed standing with Willow beside me.

Zeke looked me straight in the eye. "If you had to, could you paint a replica of *Daisies*?"

The breath whooshed out of my lungs. "Excuse me?"

He didn't repeat himself, just gazed at me levelly.

"Why are you asking?" We'd already discussed this in the context of the theft four years ago.

"Just answer the question."

I frowned and crossed my arms protectively over my chest. "I could paint something that might look like *Daisies* at first glance, but it wouldn't hold up to scrutiny if anyone took more than a couple of seconds to study it. I already told you; Bergen is a better artist than me and he's better at mimicking famous works of art. He sees it as a challenge." I glanced at Willow and muttered, "Perhaps I should have realized that was a red flag."

"Yeah," she agreed. "Maybe. But hindsight is twenty-twenty."

She wasn't wrong. I could see so many things now that I'd overlooked at the time. In the days and weeks following the Black Swan theft, I'd raked through my relationship with Bergen to uncover every one of them, and I'd beaten myself up over them mercilessly.

"Will you show me your work?" Zeke asked.

My frown deepened and I shifted uncomfortably. "Why?"

He shrugged. "So I can get a feel for it."

Or so he could figure out whether I was lying about being a forger. But whatever. I had nothing to hide.

"Everything I have is at my apartment." I'd sold off most of my work over the past four years and I hadn't created anything new. I'd tried a few times but whenever I stood at a canvas or touched a paintbrush I was brought back to the night I'd spent in that holding cell, and the awful things that people I'd thought were friends had believed about me. The gossip they'd spread. The lies the police had bought into. I could never bring myself to make more than a few brush strokes before stopping.

He got to his feet and shoved his hands into his pockets. "Let's go then."

"Call me if you need me," Willow murmured. "I can come with you now, if you'd like."

"No, but thank you. We'll talk soon."

"Keep us in the loop," Ronan called as Zeke guided me out of the office.

"I didn't do this," I muttered as soon as we were out of their hearing.

"I know." His tone was soothing, but his expression could have been carved from stone. "You should have told us about your college thesis though."

I cocked my head. "You mean the essay I wrote about *Springtime*?"

"I don't know what it was called," he replied. "But it was by Monet. You know, the same guy who made the painting you're suspected of stealing."

"It was ages ago, and studying a painting isn't the same thing as being able to reproduce it." If I were capable of creating paintings like Monet, I sure as hell wouldn't be working as a personal assistant.

"It's still relevant." His tone brooked no argument. "Is there anything else you haven't told me?"

"I'm sure there's plenty I haven't told you, but I can't think of anything that relates to the Monet." I waved my arms emphatically. "I'm not trying to hide things from you, but I had a whole career in art before I came to work here, and there could be dozens of coincidences that I haven't thought of."

"Well, if anything does cross your mind, let me know."

"Fine." I winced, hating how petulant I sounded.

We didn't talk on the journey to my apartment. When I let us in, Zeke instructed me to wait by the door while he checked each room for intruders. I didn't know who he expected to find, but he was back soon after and seemed satisfied. He locked the door from the inside.

"Show me your paintings."

"They're in the spare room." I brushed past him and headed to the smaller room opposite mine. It could be used as either a small bedroom or an office, but I used it primarily for storage. I switched the light on and carefully lifted the sheet that covered the canvases resting against one wall.

"These are all you have?" Zeke asked.

"Yeah. I sold everything else a while ago." I'd needed every bit of money I could get, and while my name had been smeared in the art world, casual buyers didn't know my reputation so it had been easy enough to sell the paintings online, although I hadn't made as much as I would have from a gallery sale with a collector who fully recognized their value. "These are the ones I couldn't sell. A couple of them were too similar to others I'd done, a couple aren't at the standard I prefer, and one I held onto for sentimental reasons. Then there's this." I picked up one of the canvases and turned it to face him. It was a reproduction of a Degas that featured young girls dancing. "Bergen challenged me to see who could make the more accurate copy. It was stupid to play along with him, but I did it anyway."

His eyebrows shot up. "That's a forgery?"

I winced. "'Forgery' is such an ugly word. It's a poor copy. I never intended for anyone to actually believe it was an original. If you see here"—I pointed near the center—"this girl is wearing a pink sash. That wasn't part of the original. It's my way of differentiating it, although any art afficionado would be able to tell it isn't actually by Degas even without the sash." I sighed. "I could copy his work all I like, but I'd never have his skill."

Zeke squinted at the painting, studying it carefully. "It's beautiful."

I laughed. "You should see the original."

"Show me."

I brought a photo of the painting up on my phone and offered it to him. "Seeing it in person is far better, but this will have to do."

He scanned the screen, then looked back at my painting and made a thoughtful sound.

"Not the same, right?" I prompted.

"No," he agreed. "But at first glance, the uninitiated might not notice the difference."

I smirked. The chance of anyone mistaking my work for a Degas was infinitesimal, but it was nice to have my ego stroked.

"Let's see the others," he said, returning my phone and turning back to the wall of canvases.

I showed him the painting I'd done of a bouquet of wild-flowers, which I hadn't felt able to sell because I'd done another of the same bouquet from a different angle. Next was the painting of the Chicago skyline that I'd botched and not been able to fix properly. He took a moment to study each, as well as the others. His gaze lingered on the final painting, an image of the mirror from my old bedroom with my reflection showing in the glass. I'd based it off a photo Bergen had snapped of me from behind, and there was something about it that meant I hadn't been able to bring myself to get rid of it.

"Jesus, Fi," Zeke breathed. "You're so talented. You should be doing this for a living, not answering phones and replying to emails."

I bit my lip and tried not to let his words get to me. I would have liked to be painting, but I'd let Bergen steal my credibility and my enjoyment of the process. Maybe there was a chance that if everything worked out, I'd be able to get it back.

ZEKE

I WAS STUNNED BY FIONA'S TALENT. I'D ALWAYS KNOWN SHE was a competent woman, but she gave the impression of being all about efficiency and realism. These paintings were something else. They had an almost dreamlike quality. And they were her leftovers. What did that say about the ones she'd sold?

"Unfortunately, there aren't many galleries who'd be willing to work with an artist with my reputation," she said ruefully.

I kicked myself. I should have thought of that before I opened my mouth. "I'm sorry."

She started to turn the paintings back around. "It is what it is."

"Wait." I touched her hand to still her, and a jolt of electricity sizzled through me.

"What?" she asked breathlessly.

I did my best to ignore the attraction zinging between us. "Do you have a signature? A way of identifying your work?"

"Here." She pointed to a small squiggle in the bottom left corner of the canvas in her hand. If I squinted and cocked my head, I supposed it looked like an F and an R.

"What about Bergen? Does he have one?"

"Most artists do." She placed the canvas down and tapped on her phone, then handed it to me. "Here." She pointed at the corner of a painting of a path through a park that filled the screen. This is his."

The signature was larger than Fiona's, and more obvious, with a looping B.

"He does this on everything he paints?" I asked.

Her lips twisted. "He did it on all of his commercial pieces, but if he was trying to pass off a forgery, he wouldn't sign it. He might have an ego but he isn't stupid."

"Would he do something to leave his mark on it though?" I was getting a feel for who Bergen Cole was, and men like him liked to put their stamp on things. Their self-centered attitude could be their downfall.

Fiona's expressive face shifted as she considered the possibility. "Maybe," she allowed. "But he already has a distinctive brush stroke pattern that isn't totally aligned with painters such as Monet. Unless he's changed that over the past four years, he would already have a signature of sorts on the forgery."

"Interesting." I leaned against the wall. "Would you recognize his work without a signature?"

She pursed her lips. "If you gave me a few paintings and told me he'd done one of them, I'd probably be able to pick it, but without any context, I doubt it."

Damn. It would have been helpful to know she could identify his work if we could somehow get our hands on a photo of the forgery from either the Monet or the Black Swan case.

I twisted one of the rings on my left hand absent-mindedly. "If you wanted to sell a piece of stolen art on the black market, how would you go about it?"

She didn't even pause to think. "I'd try to find a fence."

"Do you know any fences?" Because if she did, that would make my job much easier.

"No." She sighed. "Or at least, if I do, I don't know what they are, if you get what I mean."

"I do." I twisted the ring the other way. "I'll have my team put out some feelers. Assuming, for a moment, that Bergen has the Monet, where do you think he'd store it?"

"Somewhere with a lot of security that he controls."

"Like a bank vault?" I asked.

"God, no. Bergen is paranoid. He'd find a place no one else knew about and install the best electronic system he could find. He wouldn't want to risk even a single person knowing what he had. It would have to also be somewhere the painting couldn't be damaged. Maybe an industrial or commercial building rented under an alias, or even a second apartment, although that would be riskier if there's a chance the super might drop by."

I thought on that. If I was trying to hide a priceless painting, I'd probably choose a derelict storefront and make sure it was absolutely impenetrable. The trouble was, there were too many possibilities in Chicago for us to sift through them all, and there was nothing to say the painting was even still in the city.

Of course, if Bergen was the guilty party, and if he was as paranoid as Fiona claimed, there was one thing he'd almost certainly be doing, and that was keeping a very close eye on her.

"I have an idea," I told her. "I need you to trust me though. Can you do that?"

"Um..." She looked confused. "Like, with my life, or what?"

I shook my head. "Just stay here. I need to step outside. Don't leave the apartment. If you have to feel like you're doing something useful then write out some ideas for how you'd go about the crime if you were going to commit it."

She put a hand on her hip. "How long will you be gone?"

"Hopefully not too long." I shot her a smile. "I'm not abandoning you, okay? I'm testing a theory."

"Fine." She looked reluctant, but hey, agreement was agreement.

"Great." I backtracked out of the room. "Lock up behind me, and don't open the door without making sure you know who's on the other side."

She rolled her eyes and mock saluted. "Aye, aye, Captain."

I tapped the end of her nose. "You're so cute when you're snarky."

Her lips parted in shock. Before she could snap out a comeback, I made my exit. I waited outside until I heard the lock engage, and then glanced around. Based on what I knew of Bergen, I suspected he'd have eyes on Fiona. I walked away, hoping it looked as though I was leaving for the day, then slipped through the fire escape into a shaded alcove and waited.

Minutes passed, and I stayed as still as if I'd been carved from stone. Just when I was beginning to think I might have been mistaken, I saw movement in the alley below. A man appeared, his features hidden by a ski mask. I remained in place, waiting as he climbed the stairs, a backpack slung over one shoulder and something cylindrical clutched in his hand. The hairs on the back of my neck rose. Somehow, I knew this was our guy.

He looked up as he reached the floor beneath me and stiffened. He'd seen me.

He took off, taking the stairs two at a time. I raced after him, grabbing the handrail to make sure I didn't slip and fall. Metal clanged as the object in his hand knocked into the railing, and he glanced over his shoulder. My eyes locked on his, brown against brown, and then he tore his gaze away and leaped over the side of the railing, falling the last several feet and landing safely on the concrete. I dove after him, making it to the ground just in time to grab onto the backpack hanging off his shoulder.

He spun around and raised the object in his hand. Something flew out and stung my eyes. I squeezed them shut, but the stinging didn't ease. The backpack was yanked out of my grasp. I tried to open my eyes as I reached for him again, but they were sticky and all I could see was fog as the man in the ski mask made his escape.

10

———

FIONA

I'D JUST SAT DOWN TO RUN SOME INTERNET SEARCHES ABOUT Bergen that would no doubt prove fruitless considering how many times I'd done the same thing in the past when I heard a crash outside the apartment. I stiffened and went to the door. Was Zeke back?

I looked through the peephole and gasped. A man stood on the other side of the door, his face crimson with blood. Only the dark hair and the eyebrow piercing let me know who it was. I unlocked the door and yanked it open. Zeke tripped toward me, reaching out blindly.

"What happened?" I asked, grabbing his shoulders to steady him. I searched his face frantically, knowing he must be injured, but I couldn't find where the blood was coming from.

"I nearly had him," Zeke growled. "But he attacked me."

I touched a finger to his face and frowned. The red liquid felt tacky. I leaned closer and sniffed. He smelled of a combination of chemicals I'd recognize in my sleep.

"It's spray paint," I said. "He got you in the eyes with spray paint."

He scowled, his eyes still shut. "It fucking hurts."

I couldn't help laughing. Zeke was supposed to be this tough former spy, yet he'd been defeated by a can of spray paint.

"Are you sure it was our guy and not just someone putting graffiti on the walls?" I asked.

"I'm sure." He sounded dead serious, and since that was unusual, I believed him. "He was wearing a ski mask, and he didn't move like a kid. I don't have proof but, somehow, I just know he was our guy."

"Okay." Any lingering amusement dissipated. "I'll help you clean up in a second. I have some eyewash we can use. I'm just going to make a call."

I called Ronan and arranged for him to contact the police and to send around a laboratory technician who'd be able to check for any evidence the assailant might have left behind, then I took a quick photograph of his face before putting an arm around his shoulders and guiding him into the bathroom. Using a cloth and soapy water, I wiped most of the paint off his face and gently cleaned his eyelids, which had become partially stuck together. Once he was able to open his eyes, I found the eyewash and rinsed his eyes while he swore and muttered.

"I can't believe he caught me by surprise like that," he said as he toweled himself dry. He looked at me with red-rimmed, bloodshot eyes.

I winced. "Are you sure you don't want to see a doctor?"

He scoffed. "For a little paint in my eyes? No. They'll be fine. I'm more worried about what our spray-painter might have intended to use the paint for."

I frowned. "What do you mean?"

"I don't think it was a coincidence that you mistook it for

blood." He hesitated, then added, "I think whoever it was intended to leave you a warning message."

A shiver rippled through me. If I'd found a warning spray-painted on the door in that shade of red, it absolutely would have freaked me out. It wouldn't have taken long for me to realize it was paint, but it still would have shaken me. Honestly, even if the paint had been black, it would have still been upsetting.

There was a knock on the door and I went to answer. A Hispanic woman in a full-body hooded coverall stood on the other side.

"Hi, Amber." I greeted her with a smile. "Ronan must have sent you."

"He did." She glanced over her shoulder. "There are a couple of cops just behind me, and I don't think they're typical patrol types."

"Okay, thanks for the heads-up." I felt Zeke's presence behind me. "Zeke, can you run Amber through what happened outside? I'll try to hold off on saying too much to the police until you're back."

"Sure, but Fi, if you get the slightest impression they're looking at how they can spin this to make you seem more guilty, don't say another word."

"I won't."

He brushed past me and gestured down the corridor. "This way, Amber."

In the other direction, the elevator opened and Detectives Harrison and Goodwin stepped out. They spotted me immediately and I forced myself not to give them the evil eye. In this case, they were here to help. Theoretically. As Zeke had said, there was always a chance they'd try to spin it to make me look more guilty.

"Hello, detectives," I called. "Thank you for coming."

Neither of them smiled.

"Come in," I said as they reached my door. "Can I get you something to drink?" The longer I delayed, the better the chance of Zeke returning before we got into the nitty-gritty of why they were there.

"No, thank you," Harrison said, at the same time as Goodwin said, "A coffee would be nice."

Harrison squinted at Goodwin, who looked chastened.

"How do you take it?" I asked, leaping on the diversion.

"Black with sugar."

"Perfect. Take a seat. I'll just be a few moments."

I bustled to the kitchen and started coffee brewing—enough for two cups because Zeke might need a pick-me-up after what he'd been through. If not, then I'd happily drink it. Once the coffee was ready, I poured, added sugar to Goodwin's, and took it out. Zeke entered the apartment, looking uncharacteristically flustered, as I offered the drink to Goodwin.

"You want a coffee?" I asked him. "There's one for you in the kitchen if you do."

"No, thanks." He pushed his fringe off his forehead and dropped onto an armchair.

"What happened to you?" Harrison demanded, staring at his swollen eyes and the traces of red on his face.

I took advantage of the opportunity to slink away and fix the remaining coffee to my own liking. When I returned and sat on the other armchair, Zeke was recounting how he'd managed to stumble to the elevator and get back up to the apartment while his eyes were spray-painted shut.

"You shouldn't have cleaned up," Harrison said once he'd finished. "It makes it more difficult for us to do our job."

He smirked. "I care more about making sure I don't go blind than I do about making your job easy."

Her eyes narrowed.

"I took a photograph," I said quickly, hoping to dispel any tension.

She grunted. "Let's see."

I opened the photograph on my phone and showed it to each of them. She reached for the phone but I didn't hand it over. I couldn't be sure she wouldn't go through my messages while she was there. I didn't think there was anything incriminating, but there was no telling what they might consider "evidence."

"So, you think the fact that this person squirted spray paint in your face proves that Miss Ryan didn't steal the painting, and that the person with the paint did," Harrison said, her tone skeptical. "Is that right?"

"That's about the sum of it," Zeke agreed.

Goodwin sipped his coffee and made a sound of approval. His partner side-eyed him.

"What makes you think the assailant wasn't a run-of-the-mill tagger?" Goodwin asked.

"It's too much of a coincidence." Zeke sounded as certain as he had when I'd asked the same question earlier.

"Hm." Goodwin was clearly dubious. "This could also be something the two of you staged to throw suspicion off yourselves."

"Oh, come on!" I rolled my eyes. "You're determined to make everything fit the story you've already come up with. That isn't what happened."

"How do we know that?"

I opened my mouth to reply, but Zeke stood and gave me a look.

"Can I talk to you in the kitchen for a moment?" he asked.

"Fine." I went with him, hoping neither cop took the opportunity to look around lest they find the copy of the Degas in the spare room.

"Keep your temper in check," he murmured once we were far enough away that they wouldn't be able to overhear. "We've reported the incident, they'll have a record in their system now. They're not going to change their minds just like that, but at least we've gone through official channels so we're covered if we need to be." He held me by the shoulders and looked into my eyes. "Okay?"

I heaved a sigh. He had a point. I may have wanted a miracle, but that didn't mean I'd get one. "Okay."

ZEKE

With Fiona this close, her subtle floral scent washing over me and her dark eyes full of emotion, I wanted to wrap her in an embrace and tell her that everything would be okay. She looked so lost, and I hated seeing her like that when she was usually so fiery and put together.

Her tongue darted out to moisten her lips and heat flashed through me. Fuck, she was a sexy woman, with her full pink lips, porcelain skin, and eyes that could be doe-like if they weren't so shrewd. Her breath caught, and I wondered if she'd noticed the fact I was having trouble concentrating because of her.

"Zeke?"

"Mm?" I forced myself to raise my eyes from her mouth.

Her pupils had dilated, and the sight rocked me because it was so unexpected. I was used to being attracted to her, but she usually went out of her way to hide any answering attraction she might feel. Now, it was on full display, and I wanted to kiss her so badly.

"The police are still out there," she murmured.

"Damn." Cockblocking bastards.

I took her hand, threaded my fingers through hers, thrilled by the press of her slender hand against my larger, rougher one, and stayed at her side while we returned to finish our conversation with the police. They were still seated, and they didn't look flustered—as though they'd been conducting an illegal search while we were away—so hopefully they hadn't moved from the sofa.

"Will you be collecting evidence before you leave?" I asked, knowing I'd better warn Amber to clear out if they were. The police didn't generally like anyone interfering with a crime scene.

Harrison snorted. "Evidence of what? We could take a sample of the paint on your face, but it looks like paint and smells like paint, so I think we'll just choose to assume that it is, in fact, paint. Other than that, what else is there to look at?"

Beside me, Fiona stared at them in disbelief. I squeezed her hand, hoping she'd heed the warning not to run her mouth at them. I loved her snarky side, but this wasn't an appropriate time to let it loose.

"You could take a sample?" Fiona suggested.

"Perhaps," Harrison allowed. "We'll see if there's enough out there for it to be worthwhile."

"How about fingerprints from the fire escape?" I said. "Or he might have dropped something when he escaped?"

I hadn't noticed anything when I took Amber out there, but that was only from a cursory glance.

"The stairs from the fire escape will be covered in finger-prints," Goodwin pointed out. "The chance of us finding anything noteworthy is slim. Besides, didn't you say the guy was wearing gloves?"

Frowning, I tried to recall. He'd definitely had his head covered, but I couldn't remember whether or not I'd seen the bare skin of his hands. "I'm not sure. He had brown eyes though. You've made a note of that?"

"Of course."

Harrison stood and wiped her hands on her pants. "We have to get moving. Miss Ryan, we'll need you to be available for questioning early next week."

"You can make an appointment with my attorney," she replied.

The police left, closing the door behind themselves.

Fiona sighed. "Well, that was a waste of time."

"No, it wasn't. Reporting an incident like this is never a waste," I reminded her. "We've created a paper trail, and at some point, we might be grateful for that."

"I guess so." She looked deflated, and once again, I was struck by the urge to comfort her. Strange, when I'd never cared much about anyone else's comfort before. She glanced at me. "You still have some flecks of paint on your face. Want me to get them off?"

"Sure." I could easily do it myself, but I got the impression she needed something to distract herself, and besides, it was nice to have her fuss over me. I sat on the sofa and closed my eyes while she got a damp cloth and scrubbed at spots on my cheeks and forehead. I'd never had someone baby me. My dad had been old-school military, and my mom had decided early on that she wasn't really interested in being a parent, so tenderness wasn't something I'd experienced much. Usually, the only time anyone touched me was during sex, and while I loved that, it was different than this was. Less intimate.

I cleared my throat, concerned I might be getting a little too emotional. "We'll make them see that you're innocent."

A soft pressure landed on my cheek. Her lips. My eyes shot open just as she pulled away.

"Thank you," she said, her cheeks a rosy hue.

My stomach flipped over, and my heart ka-thunked. That kiss felt like more than a thank you. It meant something. Honestly, the past few minutes might have been the most raw connection I'd ever experienced with someone. It should have frightened me. I preferred to keep people at a distance. But for some reason, it didn't. I'd always been attracted to Fiona, but I was beginning to admire her more deeply than I'd like to admit.

I wanted her. That wasn't a surprise. But the depths of my desire for her was. I longed to kiss her again, and for this one to be completely unchaste. Was this what infatuation felt like? It wasn't as if I suddenly believed she was a perfect angel, but even her prickliness and sharp tongue called to me.

Shit.

I slid off the sofa and picked myself up from the floor. "I should go home. I'll see you in the morning."

It was already dark out, and if I was here too late, I'd be tempted to do something I shouldn't. Fiona was vulnerable right now. This wasn't the time to put the moves on her. Besides, I had no reason to think she'd be any more receptive to them now than she ever had been. She'd made her feelings toward me clear in the past. Although... I couldn't help but think something might have changed.

"Please stay," she whispered. "I don't want to be alone here, in case he comes back."

I sighed and rubbed my sore eyes. I couldn't deny her anything when she asked so sweetly. "Okay."

It was going to be a long and torturous night.

11

───────

FIONA

To my surprise, I fell asleep almost as soon as my head hit the pillow. I wasn't sure if it was knowing that Zeke was on the sofa or just pure exhaustion, but I slept through until a little after seven a.m. the next morning. Once I woke, I lay in bed for a few minutes, staring at the ceiling. Everything that had happened in the past two days felt like a nightmare—as if I could roll over, go back to sleep, and the world would be back to normal again in a few hours. How I wished that were true. Instead, I was a suspect in a massive art theft and if I didn't prove my innocence, there was a chance I'd get arrested even though I hadn't done it.

I knew what the penalties were for convicted thieves. I was looking at jail time and a fine that would set me back to where I'd started when I'd had to dig myself out of the financial hole Bergen buried me in.

With a sigh, I threw back the blankets and got out of bed. Perhaps a hot shower would make me feel better. I

92

opened the bedroom door quietly, hoping not to disturb Zeke, and stepped into the hall.

"Good morning."

I squealed, my hands flying up to cover my chest. I was wearing a nightdress, but it didn't conceal much of anything.

"Zeke!" I gasped, staring across the hall, where he was emerging from the bathroom. "I thought you were still asleep." I hadn't heard him moving around. Jesus, how sneaky was he? The back of my neck prickled. I got the feeling I really didn't want to know how he'd learned to move so silently, or what other skills he might have picked up and from where. This was a case of ignorance being bliss.

His gaze raked over me, making me hyper-aware of my state of undress. His eyes were hot, leaving no doubt what he thought of seeing me this way, and shockingly, I felt an answering tingle between my legs. Apparently, I liked him looking at me like this.

"You are the sexiest woman I've ever seen," he rasped, his hands twitching at his sides. Then he tore his eyes from me and strode briskly back to the living area. The breath eased out of me as I watched him go. For some reason, I felt disappointed that he hadn't acted on his obvious attraction. If someone had asked me a week ago whether I thought Zeke would try to get me into bed if he saw me in my night-dress, I'd have said absolutely yes, and I'd have thought poorly of him for it. Now, he seemed to be trying to keep a respectful distance and I found myself resenting it.

"You're acting crazy," I muttered to myself.

I took my time in the shower, hoping it would help me regain my composure before I faced Zeke again. I counted the length of my inhales and exhales and tried to clear my mind, but it did no good. My head was filled with a strikingly attractive smirk and hot, dark eyes.

When I'd finally dressed, gone through my limited skin-care routine, and sucked up my courage to join Zeke in the kitchen, he was once again in the process of making breakfast. This time, he clearly hadn't ordered in. He'd cooked eggs and dished up two small bowls of yogurt with fruit. Coffee was brewing, the rich scent waking me more than the shower had.

"You didn't have to make breakfast." I took one of the bowls of yogurt and looked longingly at the coffee, which wasn't ready yet.

He grinned slyly. "Did I say that was for you? Perhaps I made two bowls for myself."

I laughed, and the pressure eased from my chest. Everything was fine between us. The moment we'd shared in the hall hadn't caused any lingering tension.

"Well, now it's mine." I dunked a spoon into it and popped it into my mouth. "Seriously though. Thank you."

I'd never imagined spending this much time with Zeke before, but if I had, I'd have expected him to drive me crazy. Instead, he'd been supportive and gone out of his way to put me at ease. I gazed down at the yogurt as my stomach tightened. I was ashamed of myself for making assumptions about him, and for letting his surface-level resemblance to Bergen color my opinion of him.

Zeke ate quickly, then set up his laptop. "I've been thinking that we should see if we can trace Bergen via any credit cards or vehicles registered in his name."

I finished my yogurt and poured the coffee, passing him his and adding caramel syrup and cream to mine. "Is that something we can do?"

"It depends." He glanced at me with a raised eyebrow. "Do you want to find him ASAP, or would you rather prioritize making sure the 'i's are dotted and the 't's are crossed?"

I bit my lip, understanding what he was asking me. If he did find this information, it wouldn't be in a way that we could share with the police. We'd have to hide how we came to have it.

"Do it," I said after a moment of consideration. "If we find him, surely we can find the Monet, and at that point, it won't matter how we did it."

He pursed his lips and I got the sense he didn't totally agree, but he nodded. "We can always manufacture a trail to him some other way."

His fingers flew across the keys, and I shifted around beside him so I could see what he was doing. The interface wasn't familiar to me, but I watched him enter Bergen's name and do a search. He scanned through the results, and I followed his lead, immediately realizing that they were a list of properties registered to people named B. Cole in the Chicago area.

How had he accessed this information? I wanted to know, but at the same time, I wasn't sure I should ask. His head remained bent over the laptop as he used a filter to narrow the search. Obviously, using this interface was intuitive enough. Even I could see how it worked. But surely it wasn't something he should have had access to.

"Did you used to be CIA?" The words were out of my mouth before I could think to censor them.

His head snapped up and he stared at me for a long moment, but then his expression relaxed and he shrugged one shoulder. "I could tell you that, but then I'd have to kill you."

I chuckled, but it sounded weak to my own ears. I couldn't help thinking that despite his teasing tone, his response sounded a little too close to the truth for comfort.

ZEKE

THIS WASN'T GETTING ME ANYWHERE.

I huffed in frustration and tried another variation on Bergen's name. The problem was, he could have used an alias. There was no way to know what name he was using, or even where he was. The only reason I was coming around to Fiona's point of view about him was because of those dark eyes that had looked back at me through the ski mask, the man's build, and the fact that whoever it was had staked out Fiona's apartment. It seemed unlikely that anyone else— other than the police—would bother to do so.

My phone rang. I checked the screen and accepted the call.

"Hey, Jonah."

"Boss, I think I found something." Jonah sounded excited. To be fair, excited was his default mode, but at this point, anything was better than continuing a search I feared wouldn't lead anywhere.

"What is it?" I asked.

"There's a rumor on the dark net about an auction for stolen art happening tonight. The chatter I'm seeing says that everyone who's anyone in the local black market art world will be there."

I sat up straight. "Really? Where?"

"On a super yacht moored off Sears Bay Marina owned by a guy called Rene Laurent."

"And Rene Laurent is…?"

"The owner of a French line of beauty products. He's a multimillionaire and he's rumored to enjoy the finer things in life, including those that don't belong to him."

"Fascinating. What's Laurent doing in Chicago?"

"He's been meeting with a local perfume manufacturer.

Of course, rumor has it that's just a cover for hosting the auction."

"Interesting. Thanks, Jonah. Let me know if you find anything else about the event. Guest list. Name and description of the yacht. Whatever you can get, email it to me."

"I will."

We ended the call and I turned to Fiona. "There's chatter on the dark net about an auction of stolen art on board a super yacht owned by a French multimillionaire. Does that sound like the sort of place where someone like Bergen might try to offload a Monet?"

Fiona's eyes widened. "Yes, I'd say that's exactly the sort of place Bergen would try to sell a Monet. Not only will the people there have been vetted, but it sounds pretentious enough to appeal to him. He's always wanted to have rich connections and attend highbrow events. The only question is whether he could get in."

I rubbed my chin thoughtfully. "I'd guess anyone with a painting by an artist that famous could get an invitation if they wanted."

"Good point."

I exited the tab on the laptop, closed it, and tucked it under my arm. "We should touch base with Ronan and Kade. This could be exactly the kind of breakthrough we need."

Her smile was heartbreakingly hopeful. "You think so?"

"I do." I resisted the urge to smooth a lock of beautiful red hair behind her ear, knowing she probably wouldn't welcome my touch. "Let's go."

While we drove to the office, Fiona called Ronan to organize a meeting. When we arrived, he and Kade were already in his office. Ronan had a notepad in front of him and was twirling a pen between his fingers. Kade slouched in a chair, taking up more room than necessary. Subtlety had never been his strong suit.

We sat, and I ran them through everything Jonah had told me, which now included a description of Rene Laurent's yacht, *Claudette*, which could accommodate over a hundred people.

"We should see if we can get one of our undercover guys into the event," Kade said when I'd finished. "Someone will be catering it. If we can find out who, we can pay off one of their employees to pretend to be sick and send someone in their place."

"Not a bad idea," Ronan said.

Fiona rested her elbows on the table and leaned toward them. "Would one of your undercover men be able to identify a Monet?"

Kade shrugged. "I can show them a picture of it so they know what to look out for."

She wet her lips, her expression nervous. "But would they be able to tell if they're looking at the real deal or a forgery?"

Kade grimaced. "Possibly not."

"I could." Her words seemed unnaturally loud even in the spacious office.

"Whoa." Kade's eyebrows lowered. "You're not trained. You can't just waltz into danger like that."

I studied the determined tilt of her chin, intrigued by the idea.

"Besides," Kade added. "One of our undercover staff could slip in unnoticed. If you turned up, there's a good chance that someone would recognize you."

"So?" She arched her brow and held his gaze. I was silently impressed. The woman had a backbone of steel. "I doubt that Bergen has announced to the world that he stole it. Laurent probably knows, but as far as anyone else is aware, I'm the police's top suspect. I wouldn't be out of place among them."

"She has a point." Ronan jotted something on his paper. "Nobody would be surprised to see her."

"But..." Kade shook his head. "She has no idea how to handle herself. She'd be on a yacht in the middle of the lake. If anything went wrong, she'd be stuck."

Ronan leveled him with a look. "I'm sure you could come up with an escape plan."

"It's a bad idea," he groused.

"It's actually not." I held his gaze and then Fiona's, letting them both see that I meant it. "Especially if I go with her. I look similar to Bergen. He and Fiona have been involved in the past. What better cover?"

Kade's jaw dropped. Even Ronan looked startled. Fiona beamed at me like I'd made her day. My stomach churned. When I'd left the agency, I'd sworn never to go undercover again. Apparently, all it took was a pretty redhead to make me go back on my word.

I was screwed.

12

———

FIONA

I GLANCED AROUND THE TABLE, CONFUSED AS TO WHY KADE and Ronan seemed to be so stunned. Wasn't Zeke's background in undercover work? If so, surely it shouldn't be unusual for him to offer to go undercover with me. Obviously, it wasn't something he did at King's Security regularly, but that was just because his role as director was more about strategy and management, right?

"Are you sure?" Ronan said after a moment. "You know we'd never ask you to do anything you're not comfortable with."

Zeke nodded. "I know."

"When you came on board, you were pretty certain you never wanted to go out in the field again, and we agreed," he continued.

I looked at Zeke, surprised. I'd had no idea about that, and as Ronan's assistant, I was used to knowing everything about the company and its people.

"I can go on my own, or with someone from Kade's

team," I said, not wanting him to feel pressured into anything.

But Zeke shook his head. "I'm going with you and that's that."

I searched his eyes, hoping to get a read on what was running through his mind, but they were impenetrable. His jaw set, and there was something steely in his expression that unnerved me. I wasn't used to seeing him like this. He was usually the easygoing boss. The flirt. The man I was seeing now was someone else entirely.

That's what you get when you make assumptions.

"Is this really the best idea we can come up with?" Kade asked. "Surely there's a lower-risk alternative?"

"Sure, there is," Zeke agreed. "But it's also less likely to succeed." He twisted one of the rings on his left hand. "Like I said, I bear more than a passing resemblance to Bergen Cole, and with Fiona's help, we can close the gap so I look even more like him."

I bit my lip. For some reason, the idea of dressing Zeke as my ex made my skin crawl. I didn't want to do it. But I also knew that his suggestion made sense. Still...

"If Bergen is there in person, it won't matter how similar you look," I pointed out. "If there are two of him, it's going to raise some red flags."

Ronan grimaced. "That's a good point."

Zeke didn't seem deterred. "So, we give me another alias, and I use that if anyone asks my name, so nobody thinks I'm actively trying to pass myself off as him, but if they happen to see me and make assumptions, then that's a happy coincidence."

"What about if he confronts us?" I asked. "He'll recognize me in an instant."

"We try to locate the Monet before he does, and have an exit plan in place in case we have to make a quick escape."

"It's risky," Kade warned.

"With so little prep time and such an isolated location, any option will be risky," Zeke said. "At least, this way, the people most at risk are the ones who choose to be there knowing the full situation and potential consequences. If we were to send one of our employees, would that really be fair to them?"

Kade scowled, but he didn't argue. We all knew Zeke was right.

"So, it's settled," Ronan said. "Zeke and Fiona, you're welcome to use our supply room to choose your outfits for tonight. Meanwhile, Kade will work on an evacuation plan."

We agreed—albeit reluctantly, on Kade's part—and left Ronan's office. Zeke and I detoured past his team so he could check in on how the search for more information about the auction was going. Once he was up-to-date, we went to the supply room. My heartbeat pulsed in my ears as we entered, and when I closed the door behind us, my hands were shaking. I'd never done anything like this before. The most daring thing I'd done was pitch my work to art galleries. I'd never put my safety on the line. What if I was a terrible actress and gave us away? I'd never forgive myself if I messed up and something happened to Zeke because of it.

To distract myself, I went to a clothing rack and sifted through the options.

"For an event like this, Bergen would wear something edgy but designer," I said, my voice wobbly. "Maybe like this." I pulled out a slim-cut white suit and passed it to him, then searched until I found a dark blue shirt to go with it. "Try it with an open collar. No tie."

He smirked. "Yes, ma'am."

I ignored the jibe and scanned the selection of shoes. Most were either brown or black, but there was a pair of navy shoes made of buttery leather that would complement the look well. I placed them on the floor by Zeke's feet. "Those too."

He shucked off his leather jacket and grabbed the hem of his shirt.

"Whoa!" I exclaimed. "What are you doing?"

"Trying on the outfit." He sounded amused. "Isn't that what you told me to do?"

"Um... I..." My mouth dry, I couldn't tear my gaze from the strip of firm stomach he'd exposed above the waistline of his jeans. "I thought you'd take them to the bathroom or something."

He rolled his eyes. "If you don't want to see me then turn around."

He pulled the shirt over his head, revealing a toned torso with defined abs and an arrow of dark hair shooting downward. I swallowed. This man clearly didn't sit behind a desk all day every day. He maintained this mouthwatering body somehow.

"Fi?"

I spun around, clapping my hands over my eyes. He chuckled, and my cheeks burned. He'd caught me staring. Damn him.

"I'm ready for inspection," he said a few moments later.

I turned and gasped, the air punched from my lungs as surely as if he'd hit me. Without his signature leather jacket, he looked so much like Bergen it gave me chills. If he shaved and removed his facial piercings, they could be twins.

"It's uncanny," I whispered.

He looked uncomfortable, and I felt a flare of guilt.

I moistened my lips. "You know you don't have to do this, right?"

"Obviously."

"I mean it." I didn't want him brushing off the comment

without really thinking this through. "I don't want you to do something you'll regret for my sake. I don't know your history, but if you told Ronan and Kade you didn't want to do field work again, there must be a reason for it, and that matters." I drew in a deep breath and held his gaze. "What you want matters."

He took my hands, his fingers surprisingly rough against mine considering he spent most of his time at his computer. "I want to do this, and I'm capable of it. You don't need to worry."

———

ZEKE

I HELD FIONA'S GAZE, HOPING THAT WHATEVER SHE SAW IN mine would convince her. It helped that I sounded more certain than I felt. Honestly, I didn't know what I thought about this at all. Pretending to be someone else used to come as easily to me as breathing, but it had been a long time since I'd had to do it, and there was a good chance my skills were rusty. Not to mention there was a reason I'd sworn to never go undercover again. I'd just have to make sure Kade and I came up with a good strategy to get us the hell out of there if the need arose.

"If you're sure," she said, still scanning my face.

"I am."

I dropped her hands and looked away as memories flashed through my mind. Ernesto's sly grin as we passed each other in the halls of the building the cyber-terrorist cell we'd been embedded in used as its headquarters. It had been reassuring to know that we were both there and that we had each other's backs. Until he'd thrown me to the wolves.

"So, will this outfit do?" I asked, eager to change the subject.

"Yes." She smoothed her hands down my chest and heat flared in my gut. "If you shave, and take out the eyebrow piercing and the earring, then you should look as similar as possible."

"Great." I didn't love the idea of removing my piercings. They symbolized the changes I'd made in my life. I'd gotten the eyebrow piercing less than a week after I'd been cut loose from the agency, and the tattoos and other piercings had come soon after. I hid a smirk. At least I wouldn't have to remove *all* my piercings. There was one that Fiona hadn't discovered yet.

I undressed and rehung the clothes, smiling to myself when Fiona huffed and turned away again. My smile widened when I saw her sneak a peek.

That's right, beautiful. You can look all you like.

"Your turn," I said as I put my leather jacket back on. I'd get someone to steam the suit before we left, so it would be in the best possible condition for our night out. "Let's see what dresses we have for a glamorous yacht party."

I ran through the options. We had plenty of gala-ready designer dresses because a good-sized chunk of our clientele were rich men who didn't want to admit they needed protection, so they hired female bodyguards to accompany them to events. Of course, we'd had to make it very, very clear that our employees were security professionals and had our full authority to blacken the eye of any entitled bastards who thought they could get side benefits from the arrangement.

"What about this?" I held up a little green number that was slinky and figure-hugging.

"It's short," Fiona said, her nose crinkling. "I'll try it though."

Between us, we selected a few more options and an array of shoes.

"Let's see them," I said, not bothering to hide my enthusiasm. She was stunning, so of course I wanted her to model each of the outfits.

"Out." She pointed at the door. "I'll call you in once I'm dressed."

I left and closed the door behind me, leaning against the wall beside it. Willow walked by, her expression curious, but she didn't stop to talk. When Fiona tapped on the door and told me to come back in, I almost swallowed my tongue at the sight of her. The green dress was short, as she'd said. The hem rested midway down her slender thighs, and the neckline plunged deeper than I'd expected, giving me a tantalizing glimpse of the creamy skin of her cleavage.

"Too much?" she asked, worrying her lower lip.

I scanned her from head to toe, noting the sky-high stilettos she'd put on. "You look incredible, but we're trying to blend in and not draw too much attention. In that dress, all eyes will be on you."

She flushed, her eyes shining. She looked almost bashful. But she must know how gorgeous she was. "I'll try another," she said. "Shoo."

I left, and returned when she summoned me. The next outfit was a better fit for the occasion. She was still beautiful—she was *always* beautiful—but the dress was black and drew less attention. It sat higher across her chest, with small sleeves that made it more demure, and a skirt that swished around her knees. She'd swapped out the stilettos for a pair of kitten heels. She looked classy, but less of a stand-out than she had in the green dress.

"Perfect," I said. "We'll need to get your hair and makeup done too."

She took the shoes off and set them to the side. "I can do that myself."

"You could," I agreed. "But you shouldn't. I'm willing to bet that every other woman there will have theirs done professionally, and they'll be able to tell the difference. We need to look the part."

She sighed. "Fine. I'll arrange it as soon as we're out of here."

"Good." I stepped closer and smoothed my thumb over the line between her brows. "Are you sure you want to do this? It's not too late to change your mind."

To my surprise, she leaned into the touch.

"I'm nervous," she said. "But I can do it."

She held my gaze, and there was something so fierce about her that my heart skipped a beat. I couldn't help feeling like if I got too close to Fiona's fire, I'd end up burned. But hell, what a way to go.

I cleared my throat and pulled my hand away. "Let's get ready then."

A few hours later, we were both dressed in our chosen outfits and sitting in the back of a luxury sedan on the way to Sears Bay Marina. Kade was on standby if we needed him, and I'd assured Fiona that we wouldn't end up trapped if things went wrong. That said, she didn't know the whole plan either. I didn't want her to get into her head about it and for her worry to throw her off her game. I was confident we could pull it off, and she'd be safe. That was what mattered.

The marina was one of the smaller ones in the Chicago area, frequented only by those who could afford to pay the exorbitant mooring fees. I spotted the *Claudette* as soon as we arrived. It was one of the largest yachts present, and two men in dark suits with poorly concealed weapons stood on the dock in front of it. They must be security. According to our research, they weren't Laurent's personal employees but a local team he'd hired for the event. We'd decided it would be too risky to try to sneak past them so my team had been working on making sure we were on the guest list. Hopefully the hired security wouldn't know enough about Laurent's business or what was going on aboard the *Claudette* to be suspicious of us.

The car stopped and I turned to Fiona. "You ready?"

She was pale, but she nodded. I opened the door and got out while the driver held Fiona's door for her. Then I took her arm and mentally crossed my fingers that my team had figured out a way to get us on that list.

13

FIONA

"Oh, my God." My breath caught in my throat. "There are guards. How are we going to get in?"

Why had I not realized there would be security? It was so obvious. Of course, an event like this would be carefully protected.

I turned to Zeke, panic rising within me. He gave me a look that said to be quiet. I glared at him but didn't utter another word. He'd implied he could get us in, but I hadn't thought of this. Had he? Based on the confident way he guided me toward them, I assumed he had some kind of plan. I couldn't ask any questions without risking them overhearing so I tried my best not to look as though I was on the verge of a meltdown.

As we approached the first security guard, I realized I was hardly breathing and forced myself to inhale and exhale steadily. I'd suggested we do this. I'd volunteered for this role. I couldn't fail at the first hurdle. I plastered a smile on my face and hoped it looked real.

The man approached us, holding a tablet.

"Zane Wilson and Fiona Ryan," Zeke said, using the same tone with which he'd tell someone he wanted steak and a glass of wine.

The man checked the tablet. I squeezed Zeke's hand, certain we were going to be called out any second, but the guy waved us through. My shoulders slumped as we took the stairs onto the yacht, out of the danger zone.

"How did you do that?" I asked quietly.

"It wasn't me," he replied. "From now on, be careful what you say. You don't know who could be listening. Don't mention anything out of character."

"Got it." That would be easier for me than him because I was playing myself. I wondered who Zane Wilson was supposed to be. Was he an old alias Zeke had brought out of retirement or something new that his team had whipped up?

"This way, darling." He wrapped his arm around my waist and guided me further onto the yacht. I gazed around in awe. I'd never been on board anything like this before. I'd taken the water taxi, but the *Claudette* was on a whole other level. The yacht was so big I could hardly even feel the slight roll as it moved with the water.

We passed men and women dressed in couture. Some were elegant, but others—particularly the younger women —had miles of skin on display. I couldn't help wondering whether they were as much trophies to the gentlemen accompanying them as the Rolexes on the men's wrists. In comparison, I looked dowdy, but I supposed that was the point. We didn't want to attract more attention than necessary.

"Here, my love." Zeke took two champagne flutes from a tray carried by a passing waiter and handed me one. I didn't drink from it. I was worried enough without being impaired by alcohol. He sipped, then plucked a pair of oysters from a platter near the wall. He downed one and offered me the other. Hiding a grimace, I slurped the slimy thing and swallowed it as fast as I could. I liked most seafood, but I'd never warmed to oysters.

"Try this." The pastry was small and delicate. I tried to take it, but he held it to my lips. I bit into it. The pastry practically melted in my mouth and rich chocolate oozed from the center.

I groaned. "That's so good."

His eyes locked on my face. "Have another."

This time, I immediately took it from between his fingers, letting my tongue brush over his fingertips. Heat sparked in his dark eyes. I stared back, unable to look away until someone bumped into me from behind. I traced my lips with my tongue to make sure he hadn't left any crumbs.

"Let's look around," I said. The sooner we could figure out whether the Monet was here, the better.

We strolled into the yacht's main room, where display cases lined the walls and elegantly attired people mingled about. We took our time looking at each item. Even if I hadn't known these goods were stolen, it would have been evident soon enough. There were amulets that should have been in a museum in Cairo, paintings by lesser-known greats of the eighteenth century, and a tiara that once belonged to the Russian royal family.

"This is incredible," I breathed to Zeke. Awful, but breathtaking too. "I don't see any flower paintings though."

There were undoubtedly pieces here worth hundreds of thousands of dollars—maybe even millions—but nothing of the same caliber as the Monet. At least, not in my opinion.

"Maybe they're holding it back to use as a grand finale," Zeke murmured, his breath tickling my ear. He'd leaned close, presumably so as not to be overheard, and the sensation sent delicious tingles racing down my neck. I was sure I was blushing, but thankfully it would be difficult to tell beneath the layer of makeup.

"It's possible they've put it aside somewhere with even better security and that they'll only show it to a hand-selected group of guests with the capital to buy it," he added.

That made sense, but I was strangely disappointed. I'd hoped to see it as soon as we arrived, so I could reassure myself we were in the right place. As it was, we'd be heading out onto the water without any certainty that we weren't marching into danger unnecessarily.

"It's exquisite, no?" a woman asked in a thick French accent.

I turned, finding a pair of elegant older ladies standing beside me, gazing at the tiara.

"It's very beautiful," I agreed, since that seemed to be what they expected of me.

The taller of the pair had silver hair and cold blue eyes that flicked over me appraisingly. "It would look stunning on you, with that red hair. Will your man buy it for you?"

I pursed my lips to hold back the automatic retort that women didn't need a man to buy things for them these days. "We're in the market for something different." I exchanged a glance with Zeke, hoping he wouldn't mind me saying so. "We're art lovers."

"Ah." She smiled. "Then there are other things here that are more to your liking."

"Exactly."

She tilted her head in acknowledgment and she and her companion swept away.

"Well done," Zeke murmured. "I could be wrong, but I think that was Rene Laurent's wife. Now that she knows we're interested in art, perhaps we'll get an invitation to see the Monet."

I felt a jolt, followed by the rumble of an engine, and I automatically reached for Zeke's hand as the yacht eased into motion. My throat tightened, but then Zeke pulled me against his chest and kissed my forehead. The room began to fill with people—the ones who'd been outside coming in.

His lips moved against my skin. "Everything will be okay."

I straightened and tried to look like someone who boarded expensive yachts loaded with stolen treasures every day. God, I hoped he was right.

ZEKE

DID IT MAKE ME A BAD PERSON THAT I FOUND FIONA'S NERVES endearing? It was rare for me to see her anything other than confident, and it was nice to remember that she wasn't always the most efficient person on the planet. She was as human as the rest of us.

I edged closer, breathing her in. I loved the way she smelled, and having her nearby soothed me. I was nervous too, although I'd never let her know it. She needed me to be strong, and I could fill that role for her. After all, it wasn't as if I hadn't been in high-stakes situations before. Many had been more dangerous than this. It had just been a while since I'd experienced the wild highs and lows that came with undercover work.

A glass chimed, and I looked to the front of the room, where a man in a pinstriped suit was adjusting a microphone clipped to his collar.

"Welcome, ladies and gentlemen." His voice boomed around the enclosed space and he winced and adjusted the mic. "Sorry about that," he continued at a more reasonable volume. "As I was saying, welcome to Mr. Laurent's semi-annual auction. You'll see that we have an impressive selection to entice all comers." His smile turned sly. "There's also a private auction that will be happening near the end of the night. Some of you know what this is regarding. Others of you who are interested can ask Rene or his wife, Claudette, for a viewing at their discretion."

A faint hum swept through the room.

The speaker cleared his throat. "For those of you who don't know me, I am John Herbert and I'll be your auctioneer tonight." He checked the expensive watch on his wrist. "Please take advantage of the next fifteen minutes to view the items. Bidding will begin at eight thirty."

He switched the mic off and said something to the pudgy, balding man beside him.

"That's Laurent," I murmured, recognizing him from the photographs we'd seen earlier. My gaze wandered away from him, across the room, cataloging every person I encountered.

I stiffened. Shit. I'd hoped we'd have longer before this happened. At least long enough to confirm the presence of the Monet.

"Don't look now, but we have company."

Fiona twitched but managed not to follow my gaze. "Who?"

"Your ex." I locked eyes with Bergen Cole, who was sauntering across the room toward us, one side of his mouth hitched up as if he didn't have a care in the world. Like me, he was wearing a white suit, but his shirt was black and he wore a gold bow tie. His hair was slicked back, similarly to mine, and he was clean-shaven. I had to give it to Fiona, she'd done a fantastic job of dressing me as him.

"Well, well." He stopped in front of us, his mouth curled in a smirk, and Fiona finally allowed herself to look up. If I hadn't been touching her, I might not have noticed the way her muscles tensed. Bergen scanned me and his smirk deepened. "You certainly have a type, don't you, Fi?"

I kept my eyes on Bergen, so I didn't see Fiona's reaction, but I could practically sense the fury vibrating through her.

"He's nothing like you," she said, so levelly I was impressed. Nobody overhearing the conversation would know the depth of her emotion toward the man opposite us. I was also surprised by her words. She'd always made it clear that she didn't think much of me. Perhaps that was changing. I could only hope.

Bergen looked at me pointedly. "If you say so." He glanced toward the ceiling, and I spotted a camera not far away, presumably filming our interaction. "Being seen here won't bolster your case," he continued. "Imagine what the police would think if they saw photos of you around all of this stolen art."

I drew Fiona against my side to show my support. "If you gave the police any photos showing Fiona here, you'd also be incriminating yourself."

He shrugged. "There is such a thing as anonymous tipping." He gave Fiona a faux sympathetic smile. "You'll look terrible in orange, darling."

With that parting remark, he strode away. Fiona jerked toward him, as if she intended to chase him down and give him a piece of her mind, but I stopped her.

"Don't make a scene," I murmured near her ear, cupping her face so any onlookers wouldn't see our exchange as anything more than an intimate moment between a couple. "We need to get out of here quickly and quietly."

It was time to initiate the escape plan.

She ducked her face into the curve of my shoulder. "But what about the painting? We haven't seen it, or heard evidence that it's here. We can't go."

"It's too risky to stay now that Bergen has seen us." It was possible he'd rat us out to Laurent. I took her hand and pulled her out of the room. The guests were beginning to assemble for the auction, so hopefully they'd be distracted. I guided Fiona past the people loitering outside and around the side of the yacht, where we were alone. I pressed a button on my watch and pulled Fiona close, so that anybody who saw us would assume we'd stolen a passionate moment alone.

"Strip the dress and heels off, and jump into the water," I said softly.

She looked at me as though I was crazy. "What?"

"It's time to get out of here. I'll explain later, but we need to move fast."

Her eyes searched mine in the near-dark. "You're insane. It's going to be freezing."

I grabbed her shoulders and held her gaze. "If you trust me, jump. I promise you: everything will be okay."

When she pulled away, toed off the shoes, and reached behind herself to unzip the dress, I felt like a king. Even without the full picture, she was choosing to trust me. I'd make damn sure she didn't regret it.

In the distance, blue and red lights started flashing and a siren wailed.

"Police!" a voice hailed over a loudspeaker. "Please turn off your engine and allow us to approach."

Fiona's eyes widened, but I just nodded and waved at the edge of the yacht.

"Push off as far as you can," I said.

She swung her legs over the edge, cast one look back at

me as I shucked off my jacket and kicked off my trousers, then slipped over the edge and vanished from view. I heard a faint splash. As I hauled myself onto the ledge behind her, I checked to make sure I wouldn't land on her bobbing head, then I followed her into the dark.

14

FIONA

I GASPED FOR BREATH AS THE WATER ENGULFED ME. I SANK down, down, until my survival instincts kicked in and I started to push toward the surface. It was so cold, my chest felt as if it was being squeezed. I couldn't relax enough for the sensation to ease. My head broke through the surface and I sucked air into my lungs, filling them as much as I could, which still wasn't enough.

Something splashed into the water beside me and I mopped the spray from my eyes. A moment later, Zeke surfaced gracefully, his recovery making mine look like a fish on a hook. Why couldn't the damn man be bad at something?

A shiver wracked my body, and I became aware of the hulking form of the yacht behind me. The police sirens were still wailing and the lights had gotten much closer. The cops were on a boat of some variety and seemed to be trying to intercept the *Claudette*. Had someone tipped them off about the auction?

"What now?" I asked, struggling to breathe enough to stop myself from getting lightheaded.

Zeke tilted his head to the left. "Swim that way."

I kept my movements as soft as possible, afraid that someone above might hear us and look over. We'd been lucky that the police sirens had masked the sounds as we hit the water. If not for them, someone certainly would have noticed us slip overboard. Zeke and I gradually put more distance between ourselves and the yacht. The night grew darker as we left the glow of artificial light. As my eyes adjusted, I began to make out a shape emerging from the dark.

A dinghy.

Kade sat within it, his powerful arms rowing it toward us. When he drew level with us, he reached over the side, offering me his hand. Zeke boosted me from behind and I clambered over the edge, not even caring that I knocked my knee against the metal railing. I was so glad to see him. He gestured behind me and I turned to see a set of towels and a blanket.

I dried myself, shivering the whole time, and did my best to squeeze the frigid water out of my hair before huddling beneath the blanket. Meanwhile, Kade helped Zeke into the boat. I passed him a towel and he did the same as me, then gestured for me to let him join me beneath the blanket. He pressed up against my side and pulled the blanket around his shoulders. His body was surprisingly warm and, slowly, my shivers eased.

Kade continued to row until we were far enough away that the engine wouldn't be heard, then he turned it on and steered us toward the shore. The entire time, none of us spoke.

When we reached the shore, a car was waiting for us. I

wrapped the blanket around myself and Kade handed Zeke a towel, which he slung around his waist.

"What just happened?" I was bewildered.

"That wasn't really the police," Zeke replied, sounding a little smug. "It was a diversionary tactic so we could escape. I have an alert button on my watch and when I pressed it, Kade knew to activate the extraction plan."

"You couldn't have told me what to expect?" I asked as we got into the car.

"You were scared enough," Kade said. "We didn't want to worry you when we knew it might not come to anything. It was a simple plan and Zeke knew he could execute it without you being aware of it beforehand."

I narrowed my eyes, suspecting that Kade had been the one who'd made that decision. He could be overprotective, especially when it came to women. I liked to think Zeke respected me enough to have told me otherwise. Of course, he could have said something even if Kade didn't like it and he'd chosen not to.

Nope, I was angry with both of them.

"I'd have liked a say in the matter," I said. "Besides, isn't it illegal to impersonate the police?"

The car started moving, and the driver cranked the heat up—a fact I was grateful for.

Zeke shrugged. "Following the rules has never been my thing."

I looked at Kade. While Zeke wasn't the best rule-follower, Kade historically had been. At least, other than the time he'd gone rogue when Sage was in danger, and really, who could blame him for that?

Kade's expression turned sheepish. "Sometimes there's room for exceptions."

Right.

"So, are we going back to the office?" I asked. I really wanted to get Zeke alone and demand some answers.

The men exchanged a glance.

"We're going to a safe house," Zeke said. "Just in case anyone is tracking us. It's unlikely, but better safe than sorry."

"Will there at least be a change of clothes for me there?" I couldn't believe they'd organized all of this behind my back. It hurt. I'd thought we were a team, but they were acting as if I were just a child to shepherd around. I had less experience than them, but I was smart and I could be practical. They didn't have to treat me like I was made of glass. Or as if they didn't trust me. I'd had enough of that in my life. Nobody had trusted me after the accusations the police spread four years ago, but I'd thought these men were different.

"Yes," Zeke said. "We had a bag packed for you."

"Of my things or stuff from the company?"

"Your things," he replied. "We sent one of the women on Kade's team to do it."

I relaxed slightly. At least it had been a woman. I hated to think of one of the big, muscled male bodyguards pawing through my underthings.

I was silent for the rest of the trip, while Zeke debriefed Kade on everything that had happened on board the *Claudette.* I held myself apart from them, warm enough that I didn't need their body heat. Eventually, we pulled up outside a residential apartment building not too different from my own.

"You two head in," Kade said. "I'll go back to the office and update Ronan."

"Thanks for the rescue," I said, because however I might feel about being kept in the dark, I owed him that. If he hadn't been so fast to scoop us out of the lake, I could have hypothermia now instead of being mildly pissed.

"No problem." He gave me a tentative smile. "Stay safe, okay, Fi?"

"I'll try." I imagined that tonight was the most excitement I'd see in my life. I almost smiled. Who'd ever have expected no-nonsense Fiona to jump off the side of a French millionaire's yacht at night? Not me, that's for sure.

Zeke thanked Kade too, and we got out of the car. I pulled the blanket closer around myself, and he did the same with his towel. We both looked bedraggled, but fortunately, there wasn't anyone around to stare. Zeke led me to an apartment on the ground floor and slotted a key into the lock. I hadn't noticed Kade give it to him, but I'd also been preoccupied, so perhaps that wasn't surprising.

As soon as we were inside, Zeke flicked the lock into place and pulled his wet top off over his head. I turned to face him and put my hand on my hip.

"Why couldn't we have stayed on the yacht a few more minutes, just to try to set eyes on *Daisies*?"

ZEKE

Fiona looked like a water sprite. The water had darkened her hair to the color of blood, and her skin was pale except for the soft pinkness of her mouth and the freckles that stood out starkly across her nose. I'd never seen her more beautiful.

"What Bergen said about the police made me think he was up to something," I said. It hadn't only been that. I'd gotten a vibe from the guy that I couldn't quite explain.

"Whether it was getting the security footage to implicate you, or whether that was just a distraction while he told Laurent there were uninvited guests aboard his yacht, I'm not sure. I didn't want to run the risk of giving him the time to make a move."

I'd never have been able to live with myself if Fiona and I had been captured and she'd suffered as a result. Perhaps I'd been overly cautious, but I'd gambled with my safety in the past and lost. While I'd survived, it certainly hadn't been without scars, and I wanted better for Fiona.

"I..." I trailed off and cupped her face in my palm. She looked up at me, her eyes luminous. "I couldn't take the chance that anything might happen to you."

I had no idea how she would react to my confession. I'd never been so vulnerable with her before. I didn't expect her to grab my shoulders, pull me in, and kiss the crap out of me, but that's exactly what she did. Without any warning, her lips were on mine. They were cool and yielded where our mouths met.

"You sweet, aggravating man," she gasped as we separated. "You drive me insane, but then you go and say something like that."

I gathered her into my arms, needing another taste of her. My tongue delved into her mouth, exploring her, and she pressed against the planes of my body, somehow both soft and strong at the same time.

"Thank you." She pulled back and nuzzled the side of my neck. "I'm pissed that you didn't tell me the whole plan, but thank you for having my back."

My heart warmed. "If it helps, we didn't tell Ronan either, so he has plausible deniability if we get into any trouble."

She shook her head. "You're a surprisingly decent man."

"Surprisingly?" I arched a brow, my tone teasing. "Didn't you always know I was wonderful?"

She rolled her eyes. "And so humble."

"You know it." Despite the flippant words, my heart was pounding wildly, and I had no doubt she could feel it through the thin blanket that separated us.

"I'm going to have a shower," she said, drawing away.

I swallowed my disappointment. I'd thought something was happening between us, but perhaps not. "Sure. I'll go after you."

"Or," she said pointedly, "you could join me."

"*Oh.*" Yeah, that sounded much more like it. I grinned. "You have such good ideas."

She grabbed my hand and dragged me to the two doors that came off the open-plan living area. Behind one was a bedroom with two full-size beds, and the other had a tiled floor and an open shower with a toilet hidden in the back corner.

"Perfect." She dropped the blanket and started the shower, then turned to face me wearing nothing but her panties and a bra. My jaw dropped. She'd stripped earlier, but I hadn't been able to appreciate the view. Now, there was nothing to stop my eyes from lingering on her narrow waist, high breasts, and slender thighs. Holy crap, she took my breath away. As I watched, she peeled down the panties, revealing a smooth pussy that made my mouth water.

"Let me help you with that." I stepped forward and flicked the hooks of her bra open, sliding my hands around to cup her flesh and toy with her nipples. She whimpered and leaned back against me. My cock throbbed, already hard and ready to join the party. After taking a dip in chilly Lake Michigan, I was afraid my balls might have climbed up inside me permanently, but it seemed like I needn't have worried.

I rubbed my thumbs over the sensitive tips of her nipples, forming them into stiff peaks. She turned in my arms, wriggled her tight little ass against my cock and made a soft sound of approval. I tilted her head to the side and kissed the length of her neck, sucking a mark onto the creamy skin at the crook of her shoulder. She turned in my arms and pushed both the towel and my briefs down over my hips. My cock slapped against my lower abdomen and stood at attention.

"Oh, my God." Her lips parted and her pupils dilated as she stared down at my cock. "It's pierced."

"So it is."

She reached toward it, then paused. "Can I?"

"Go ahead."

She traced her finger along the curved Prince Albert piercing, her eyes growing wider every second. "Didn't that hurt?"

I shrugged. "Only for a while."

At the time, I'd had other things on my mind, so a little pain in my cock head had hardly registered.

"How does it feel... inside?" The question emerged in a breathy whisper.

I grinned. "It hasn't been inside me, so I don't know. There's only one way to find out."

She raised her eyes to mine, and they burned with naughty promise. "I intend to."

She plastered herself against me, but just as her lips were about to touch mine, I experienced a pang of conscience.

"Wait." I held her close but angled my face down, my forehead still against hers, so I'd be less tempted to kiss her. "You're hopped up on adrenaline."

I didn't want anything that happened between us to be something she'd regret later.

With two of her fingers, she tilted my chin up. Her mouth hovered over mine, and then her teeth sank into my lower lip. When she pulled away, she was smiling with satisfaction.

"That's what you get for implying I don't know what I want," she snarked. "If you don't want me, just say it, but if you're pulling some kind of weird, last-minute gentleman act, stop it. I don't want you to be a gentleman. I want you to do filthy things to me."

Despite my shock, I smiled. Who the hell would turn down an offer like that?

15

FIONA

Zeke kissed me like nothing else existed. Not the stream of hot water behind us, or the discarded towel on the floor by his feet, or the specter of the stolen Monet hanging over our heads. His kiss consumed me until everything around us blurred and all I knew was the slide of his tongue against mine and the insistent throbbing between my legs that said I wanted to discover how that Prince Albert piercing felt sooner rather than later.

I felt warm water on my back and realized that he'd guided me into the shower. I tilted my head back to let the water run through my hair, and he latched onto my throat, kissing and nibbling his way from the base to my jawline. He squirted shampoo onto his palm, rubbed his hands together, and massaged it into my hair. My eyes closed and I groaned. God, that felt good. His firm fingers dug into the tense knots at the base of my skull.

"You are so good at that," I murmured.

He rinsed the shampoo out of my hair and applied

conditioner. Next, he started to wash me. My limbs turned to jelly beneath his ministrations and it was all I could do to stand there and let him soap me. Once I was clean and smelled of roses rather than the lake, I grabbed the shampoo to return the favor. I had to stretch to lather his head, but it felt lovely to run my fingers through his hair and sense the tension ease from his body. I'd had sex less intimate than the experience of washing his hair.

He put his head under the water to wash out the shampoo. When he emerged, sputtering, I gently mopped the water from his eyes and started to massage soap into his firm, inked chest. The tattoos I'd caught glimpses of were on full display now. They flowed across his chest and down his arms, and on his back, a snake coiled around a scepter. It looked so lifelike I thought it might open its eyes at any second and hiss at me.

I eyeballed his cock, which was still hard. I was tempted to get to my knees and explore the piercing with my tongue, but my legs were shaky and I didn't know if they'd hold me up.

"Bed?" I asked.

He flashed me a grin. "Hell, yeah."

I turned off the shower and grabbed one of the fluffy towels hanging over the railing, handing the other to Zeke. We dried quickly—and not particularly thoroughly—and raced to the bedroom. I flopped onto one of the beds and Zeke lowered himself over me, inserting his legs between my thighs and nudging them apart. His erection pulsed over my sex and ground into me as he let me take some of his weight. I arched against him, sighing. It felt so good.

I hadn't been with anyone for a long time, so I was coiled tight and primed to spring at the slightest touch. Zeke kissed me, his lips teasing mine while he rocked against me, fanning the flames of my desire.

"You have such a pretty pussy," he murmured against my mouth. "Can I taste it?"

"Oh, yeah."

I shuddered as he scooted down my body and settled his mouth over me. There was no gentle easing into it. He feasted on me like I was his favorite dessert. Throwing my head back, I cried out.

"That's it, beautiful," he growled. "Let me hear what I do to you."

He tongued my clit, sucked, and used his mouth until I was writhing, my hands buried in his damp hair, pleading words spilling from my lips.

"Mm." He raised his head and looked up at me, then licked his lips.

The heat within me coiled tighter.

"Oh, God," I whimpered.

"You're decadent, Fi."

"I need you," I whispered. I'd deny that I'd said it until my dying day, but if he didn't fill me right then and there, I might have screamed.

His expression softened. "You have me." He sat back on his haunches and looked around, then his face seemed to freeze. "Uh, Fi, do you have a condom?"

I felt like face-palming. "Of course. I always keep a condom on me when I strip off my clothes and jump off a yacht in the middle of the night."

He looked at me fondly. "Maybe you should."

I bit my lip to keep from laughing. "Maybe." I waved toward the nightstand. "In there?"

He checked. "No. I guess most people have other things on their mind when they're staying here."

He climbed over me again, his cock pressing against the juncture of my thighs, and I rocked toward him instinctively.

I needed to come. It wouldn't take much. I didn't think I'd ever been so desperate before.

"I had a test after Bergen," I blurted. "I'm negative. I'm on contraception, and I haven't been with anyone since then."

His eyes widened, his pupils blowing out. "Are you saying you'd let me take you bare?"

"If you're safe too." I bit my lip, knowing it might be a non-starter. No doubt he got far more action than me.

"I was tested last month," he said thoughtfully. "I haven't had sex since the test."

"Really?"

He winked. "Rumors of my whorishness are, unfortunately, exaggerated."

Yet another way I'd gotten him wrong. Would I never cease making mistakes when it came to Zeke Watts?

"Then fuck me," I said. "Prove to me that not all of the rumors about you are false."

His grin spread, and while it was as teasing as ever, honest joy shone in his eyes too. "Challenge accepted."

He fitted himself against me and pushed in an inch at a time, waiting for me to adjust. I stiffened at first, unused to the intrusion, but then the cool metal of his piercing bumped against the inside of my channel and I gasped. Oh, that had potential. When he was seated fully inside me, he captured my mouth in a thorough kiss that left me breathless and my lips slightly swollen.

He drew back and thrust deeper. I clutched his shoulders and wrapped my calves around the backs of his thighs, urging him on. He moved faster, winding me tighter, like a thread about to snap. I heard myself murmuring nonsense words and making sounds of pleasure as he filled me again and again. It felt incredible to have him like this. His dark eyes burned as he gazed down at me, and I found myself unable to look away.

"Are you going to come for me, beautiful?" he asked, never taking his eyes off me. I could see the pleasure in his, and it thrilled me to know he felt that because of me. I'd done that to him. I was the reason this enigmatic man was coming undone.

"I'm so close," I panted.

He kissed me again, and his pelvis ground into my clitoris. Sparks exploded behind my eyelids and I shook as I fell apart beneath him.

"That's it," he said. "You're fucking perfect."

His thrusts became erratic and then he stilled, pulsing inside me. Feeling him come without a condom was intense, and an aftershock rippled through me. He flopped to the side, being careful not to crush me. I hesitated for a moment, debating whether to clean up, but then he pulled me into his arms and settled me against his chest.

"Stay," he said, his voice rich with satisfaction. "Right here."

* * *

ZEKE

There was nothing quite like waking with an armful of beautiful woman, the scent of sex still hanging in the air. I grinned, feeling lighter than I had in years, and pressed a kiss to Fiona's forehead. She mumbled something sleepily but otherwise, didn't stir. Carefully, and reluctantly, I untangled myself from her. I had no regrets, but I also didn't know what this meant. I did know that Fiona wasn't the type of woman who'd mess around with someone for the hell of it —provided, of course, that her decision-making hadn't been blunted by adrenaline. I also knew that she'd jumped off the side of a yacht into deep, cold water purely because I'd said to.

She trusted me, and that made my heart feel two sizes too big.

Not only was my trust rarely given, but few people ever fully trusted me in return. Ronan did. I thought Kade might too, although I could never be certain with him. But Fiona's trust was an unexpected gift, and I intended to protect it. I wouldn't give her any reason to doubt me.

I edged from the bed and stood over her for a moment, taking in the contrast between her fiery hair and her pale skin. Even in sleep, she was vibrant. Unable to resist, I stroked the backs of my fingers across her cheek, then bent and kissed her shoulder. I pulled on a pair of track pants and a t-shirt, grabbed my phone, which Kade had given me last night before we parted ways, and left the room before she woke. I closed the door behind me.

Kade sat on the sofa, a mug of steaming yellowish liquid on the coffee table in front of him. I wasn't surprised. I'd heard him come in earlier, but I hadn't wanted to leave Fiona. Moments like that were meant to be cherished. He gave me a look that said he had a pretty good idea of what I'd been up to. He didn't comment on it though. In some ways, his silence was harder to handle.

I sighed and tugged my hand through my rumpled hair. "Don't give me that look. I have no idea what we're doing, but I promise, I won't hurt her."

He nodded. "She's been through enough."

I went to the kitchenette and searched the cupboards. There was no good coffee, just the instant stuff. I made a cup anyway. Caffeine was definitely called for this morning.

"What's that?" I asked, gesturing to his mug.

His face crinkled with distaste. "Some kind of herbal tea

that Sage is convinced is better than coffee for waking you up."

I sat kitty corner to him, on an armchair. "What's the verdict?"

"It tastes fucking awful, so I suppose you could say it's enough to shock someone awake."

I chuckled and sipped my shitty instant coffee. Kade was so gone for his girl. He'd probably drink green smoothies for breakfast if she decided that was what he needed. It was sweet, and usually, I'd give him hell for it, but today, I wasn't in the mood to rile him up.

"Do we have any orders from the boss man?" I asked.

He shook his head. "Just to keep him in the loop."

"Easy." Although I didn't intend to mention the personal development between Fiona and me. At least, not yet. Hopefully Kade would keep it to himself too. I checked my phone, but there were no messages. "Have you heard whether the auction went ahead last night after our interruption?"

"No." He scowled. "No one would tell me anyway. They'd have gone straight to you or Ronan."

"True enough." After all, it was my team who'd be scouring the dark net for updates. "No issues with the police?"

"No, thank God." His upper lip curled, he sipped the tea and set it down with a shudder. "I don't even want to know what's in that."

"She didn't tell you?"

He pursed his lips. "She might have, but I was probably distracted."

I hid a smile. I'd bet he was. One look in her big eyes and he became blind and deaf to the world.

Across the room, the bedroom door opened and Fiona padded out, wearing a cotton King's Security t-shirt that hung to her thighs. Her hair was mussed and she squinted at us blearily. I half-expected her to squeal and run back to the room when she spotted Kade—either because of the embarrassment of having him see her like that, or because she was ashamed of the fact her casual attire made it even more obvious we'd slept together. But instead, she smiled, walked straight over to me, and dropped onto my lap.

She looped her arms around my neck and kissed me. "I'd have preferred it if you were still in bed when I'd woken up," she murmured.

My heart filled. I drank in the sight of her gorgeous face, with those endearing freckles across her nose, and the tilted edges of her smile. She wasn't ashamed of what we'd done, and she didn't regret me. Fuck, I was amazed at how good it felt to know that.

"Next time, I'll do better," I promised.

Kade cleared his throat. "Sorry, Fi, that was my fault."

She rested against my chest and tucked her legs up as she angled herself toward him. I smoothed down the t-shirt to make sure Kade didn't get an eyeful of anything she wouldn't want him to see. Having her close to me like this was right. Every part of me knew it.

"So," she said, sweeping that glorious hair over her shoulder. "Do we know where Bergen is?"

16

———

FIONA

Kade looked at Zeke with surprise in his eyes. It made me suspicious.

Zeke cleared his throat. "I, uh, messed with his phone yesterday and was able to remotely activate a location tracker, so provided he hasn't destroyed it, we should be able to find out exactly where he is."

I stiffened and removed my arms from around Zeke's neck. "You're tracking him?"

"Yes." He sounded hesitant, perhaps sensing my mood.

I looked him in the eyes. "Is there a particular reason why we didn't follow him last night?"

He looked steadily back. "My team had instructions to monitor his whereabouts. They know exactly where he's been since we left the yacht. If he went anywhere that raised alarm bells, they would have alerted us. We needed to rest last night. There was no point in following him then. The whole point of a tracker is that we don't have to tail him in person."

I gritted my teeth. I could see where he was coming from, but I was sick and tired of being kept in the dark. Especially when Kade's surprise led me to think he assumed Zeke had told me this already.

"Is there a reason you didn't let me know about this yesterday?"

He shifted his weight, seeming uncomfortable for the first time. "You have a lot riding on us proving that your ex stole the Monet. I thought you'd insist on following him even though, as I said, it wouldn't have achieved anything."

My jaw was beginning to ache. "So, what you're saying is that you knew I'd have a different opinion from yours, and you didn't want the hassle of having to discuss it with me."

"Fi." Zeke cupped my face, and I was surprised to realize that his signature rings were missing from his hands. Perhaps he'd lost them in the lake last night. "I'm sorry you're upset, but it was the best tactical decision to make."

"You kept me in the dark." My voice was thick, and I felt like crying. Once again, someone had proved they didn't trust me. I thought we'd turned a corner after yesterday, but actions spoke louder than words, and Zeke's were telling me not to rely on him to treat me like an equal.

"I'm sorry."

I could hear his remorse, but I also got the impression that if he had a do-over, he wouldn't change anything.

"Don't be upset." Kade sounded pleading. "You know I can't handle sad women."

I rolled my eyes, but on some level, I knew that however upset I was, it wouldn't move us forward. If I wanted to nail Bergen, other things were more important than my hurt feelings.

Zeke's phone rang. I got off his lap and sat on the sofa while he answered.

"What's up, Ellie?" he asked, then tapped at the screen.

A moment later, Ellie's voice filled the room. She was one of Zeke's best people, and I'd always liked her.

"The auction was canceled last night," Ellie said. "After the scare with the 'police,' they headed back to shore and went their separate ways. Rene and Claudette Laurent have already booked flights back to France. They leave in a few hours."

"What about the Monet?" Zeke asked. He caught my eye, and I got the impression that his putting this call on speaker phone was an apology for the things he hadn't told me. It wasn't enough, but it was a start.

"There's a rumor about someone holding private viewings of the stolen Monet for anyone who was at the auction and missed out on the chance to see it," Ellie replied.

"Do those rumors tie back to Bergen Cole?" he asked.

"Unfortunately not. It's all very vague. There are no names directly linked to it at this point, and there's no viewing address or means of contact either, but we'll keep looking."

"Thanks, Ellie. Let us know as soon as you find anything," Zeke instructed.

"On it, boss. Talk later." She hung up.

Zeke faced Kade and me. "We should check Cole's current location and see if he's been anywhere that would make a good storage location."

"Yes." I was relieved to know we'd actually be doing something to make progress. What point was having the ability to track Bergen if we did nothing with it?

"Kade, did you bring my laptop?" Zeke asked.

Kade went to the kitchen counter and opened a black case, extracting a slim laptop from it. He handed the laptop to Zeke. "Let's find this bastard."

ZEKE

I'D NEVER REALIZED FIONA WAS SO IMPATIENT, BUT IF I'D learned one thing today, it was that. We'd spent hours monitoring her ex's location on the laptop. At first, she'd been engrossed, but she'd gradually grown frustrated with how slowly everything moved. Bergen had spent an hour at a cafe for breakfast, then returned to a residential complex—my team were looking into whether it was his apartment building—for another couple of hours.

When he'd gone into motion again, Fiona had been excited, practically vibrating as she sat next to me, only to slump when he entered a restaurant she said used to be one of his favorites.

Another hour passed. Kade had left not long after we started our cyberstalking, and Fiona didn't seem to appreciate my amusement at the way she was pacing and muttering, desperate for something to happen.

"This is so boring," she complained forty minutes into Bergen's restaurant visit. "I thought spying on people was supposed to be thrilling."

I laughed, smiling at how put out she sounded. With her lower lip set in a sulky pout, she was adorable.

"Most surveillance doesn't keep you on the edge of your seat," I said. "At least we can do this from the comfort of the apartment so you can pace all you like. Could you imagine if we were stuck in a car together watching him?"

She grimaced. "Okay, good point. But surely he has better things to do than eat. The man has a stolen painting worth millions. If that were me, I wouldn't be going out for brunch with my friends."

"All the better to throw suspicion off," I said.

"What suspicion?" She threw her hands up. "The only

ones who suspect him are us, and we don't have the ability to arrest him, so why would he care?"

I leaned back against the sofa and eyed her thoughtfully. "So, your problem is that you're bored?"

She sighed and pushed her hair off her forehead. "I'm sorry, I just wish he'd do something that would distract me from what he said yesterday about me being in an orange jumpsuit."

I felt a pang of sympathy.

"Hey." I waited for her to look at me. "It's going to be all right. And if you need a distraction, I have just the thing." I waggled my eyebrows suggestively and she laughed. That laugh made me feel like a king.

"I need to find something to keep my hands busy," she said. "Do you have any paper?"

I gestured toward the case on the counter. "Look in there."

She checked inside and pulled out a pad of blank notepaper and a pencil. Then she sat at the end of the sofa, her feet tucked beneath her, and started scribbling. I checked the screen to make sure Bergen hadn't moved, although it wasn't really necessary since I'd set an alert to ping if he was in motion for more than a few minutes.

I lit my phone screen to see if I had any messages, but there were none, so I opened my work inbox and began looking through the emails I'd received for our other, more routine jobs. Benson had been handling the bulk of those. I really needed to update his job title from assistant to something more fitting of what he actually did. Without him, my life would be infinitely more difficult.

I finished replying to an email about a potential new client who Benson thought sounded dodgy, then glanced at Fiona. She'd showered and gotten dressed a while ago, much to my disappointment, and now her hair spilled over her shoulders like fiery silk while the pencil whizzed across the page. Her forehead was crinkled with concentration and her lower lip was caught between her teeth.

Something inside me settled. If I could see her like this every day, I'd be happy. Unfortunately, I had some ground to make up because it had been obvious she was angry about the decisions Kade and I made without consulting her. I could see her perspective, and I hated the thought that she might believe I didn't trust her judgment, but I also knew that we'd had reasons for making those choices, and our reasons were valid regardless of Fiona's feelings.

"What are you doing?" I asked, curious.

She looked up, blushing slightly, and angled the notepad toward me. She'd sketched me standing in the narrow alley on the side of the yacht, where I'd told her to strip and jump. My face was shadowed, my mouth smirking, and tattoos peeped out from between the open buttons of my shirt. Behind me, a few stars spotted the sky. But what really caught my attention wasn't the drawing itself, but the way she'd captured my mood on paper. She hadn't just reproduced my face; she'd illustrated my soul. The dark parts of it, the dirty parts of it, and the parts I sometimes allowed to be hopeful.

Emotion clogged the back of my throat. From this one single sketch, I could tell that she saw me. More than anyone else had in a long time.

"It's amazing," I said. "You're very talented."

She cocked her head, eyeing me curiously. "It's all right. It needs a lot of polishing."

I rubbed my hand over my mouth, unable to take my eyes off it. "You're too hard on yourself. Really, it's... something else."

Her eyes narrowed. "Are you trying to butter me up?"

"No." I checked the screen one last time and went over to her, dipping my head to kiss her cheek. "You're incredible."

"Yeah?" Her smile was shy.

I started to draw back but she grabbed me and pulled me closer, kissing me on the mouth. I groaned and tasted her lips. She came up onto her knees, her hands wandering down my chest. I wanted to scoop her into my arms and carry her to the bedroom, then drop her on the bed and make her beg for my cock, but before I could do anything, a ping sounded from behind us.

Fiona drew back. "He's moving."

17

FIONA

I HURRIED TO THE LAPTOP AND WATCHED THE LITTLE DOT THAT represented Bergen move steadily down the street and around a corner. He was moving quickly enough that he must be in a car. He traversed the city, pausing in a few places, but not for long enough to suggest he'd actually gotten out of the car. He was probably just stuck in traffic in the busier areas.

Zeke sat beside me and we didn't speak until Bergen finally came to a stop in a run-down commercial area. I brought it up on Google maps and looked at the satellite imagery. Several storefronts were boarded up, with only a vape shop and a convenience store that seemed to be open to the public—assuming the images were up-to-date.

"I have a better idea," Zeke said.

He navigated away from the satellite imagery and switched through a few tabs, typing furiously. In a few minutes, a series of camera displays filled the screen, each of them showing a different angle on what appeared to be the same street.

"How did you—"

"Don't ask," Zeke cut in. "It's best if you don't know."

I frowned, but when Bergen appeared on screen, I didn't pursue the matter. My ex looked different from yesterday. He wore a sports jacket with a woolen hat pulled over his head and a scarf twisted around his neck. Only a slice of his face was visible between the scarf and the hat, but I'd recognize him anywhere. His jeans were scuffed, and he kept his head low as he hesitated, glanced around, and went to one of the boarded-up shops. He unlocked the door and let himself in.

"That's got to be it," I exclaimed. "That's where he's keeping the painting."

"We can't know that for sure," Zeke replied. "But it does seem suspicious."

I stood. "Then let's go."

He leaned back against the sofa and laced his hands together behind his head. "Go where?"

"To catch him in the act." I waved at the computer screen. "This is the perfect time. If we go now and prove that he has it, the police will be able to arrest him and get it back."

Every minute we weren't getting closer to that shop was a minute wasted.

"We need to wait." His tone was blunt, but his expression was apologetic. "We don't want to rush in without a plan, and without knowing what kind of protective measures he has in place. The building might be alarmed, or he could have an armed guard. By the time we get there, he could be gone. It would take us a while to travel over, and he may not intend to stay long."

"But what if he moves it again?" I couldn't believe we

were just going to sit here and let him do whatever he wanted.

"Then we'll track him and see where he takes it," Zeke said, far too reasonably. "We have the upper hand because he doesn't know that we know where he is. He's probably on edge after the incident on the yacht. If we wait another day, he might let his guard down. It's important that he doesn't know we're coming."

My chest felt hot and tight. I wanted to argue, but as much as I hated to admit it, he was right. I'd been so hung up on wanting him to trust me, but in order for that to happen, I had to make trustworthy decisions. I couldn't allow my years of festering anger to take the lead.

"Okay," I said. "When would you recommend going there?"

His smile loosened the tension in my chest. "Tomorrow night. In the meantime, we'll keep an eye on anywhere else he goes in case he leads us somewhere even better."

I gritted my teeth at the thought of delaying for so long, but I managed to keep my impatience in check. "Should we tell the police? It would be nice to give them a lead to follow that doesn't come back to me."

"How do you suggest we tell them we got the information?" Zeke asked. "Tell them we tampered with his phone and added an illegal location tracker?"

"What about an anonymous tip?" If Bergen could threaten me with that, surely we could return the favor.

"At this point, I doubt anything we give them will be enough for them to act on. If we wait until tomorrow, we can at least give them a firsthand account rather than a guess."

I rubbed my temples, my head beginning to ache. I'd often believed Zeke did whatever he liked and dealt with the consequences later. It would seem I'd been wrong, because I really wished he'd do that now, but I could tell he wasn't going to budge.

"So until tomorrow night, we just sit here and watch a dot move around on a screen?" I let frustration enter my voice.

"And we make plans so we don't end up in hot water," he said.

I growled. I understood the need for delay, but I didn't like it.

"Hey, it's not all bad." Zeke's voice was teasing. He pushed the laptop aside and dropped to his knees in front of me, bracketing me between his arms. "It means we get to spend more time together."

"I suppose so," I allowed, heat blossoming low in my core.

His hands traveled up my legs, to the tops of my thighs. "I bet I could distract you."

I smiled slowly. "I wouldn't mind if you did."

"Nope." He sat back on his heels and smirked. "I need enthusiastic participation or none at all."

"Fine," I huffed. "Please distract me, Zeke. I want it."

"That's more like it."

He pushed my skirt up to reveal my panties. Whichever woman had packed my bag had opted to include my more sensible pairs—a smart call, but I couldn't help wishing Zeke could see me in lace. I raised my hips and he pulled them down. He hovered above me, his breath teasing my oversensitive flesh. His tongue darted over me and I gasped, my hips instinctively chasing him.

He licked me again, with more pressure. I relaxed against the sofa and enjoyed the play of his tongue over me, and the way his lips rubbed my clit. Even though he'd shaved yesterday, his cheeks were stubbly already and the rasp of them felt wonderful against my thighs.

He sucked his finger into his mouth, then worked the wet digit inside me. When he stroked me and made love to me with his tongue at the same time, I lost my mind. I arched toward him, begging mindlessly. He hummed his approval and the vibrations made me groan.

When he stopped, I cried out in protest.

"Whose mouth is on you?" he demanded.

I stared at him in confusion. "Well, yours *was*."

"Exactly." He grinned. "Mine. Not Bergen's. I'm not him. You get that, right?"

"I do," I said. "I promise. Please don't stop."

"Never."

He gave me what I needed, murmuring how beautiful I was and how much he wanted me. When a wave of pleasure washed through me, my limbs tingling pleasantly, I sighed his name, and I could have sworn I heard him whisper something in response, but in my blissed-out state, I couldn't understand the words.

ZEKE

I was achingly hard, but I tried to pull away as Fiona came down from her post-orgasm high. I'd successfully distracted her, but I needed to keep my distance or I'd go overboard. I couldn't think straight when I wanted her so badly.

"Don't." Her fingers tightened in my hair. "I can sense you retreating."

I nuzzled against her. "Not for good. You need a moment to catch your breath." And I needed to remember that she wasn't mine yet, as much as I might want her to be.

"No, I don't." She smiled lazily. "That's just you thinking you know what's best for me. What I actually need is your cock in my mouth."

My cock throbbed. It liked that idea. Fuck. I didn't ask if she was sure, because if I'd learned one thing about Fiona, it was that she didn't like to be questioned when she'd already made her thoughts clear. Besides, what kind of moron would I be to turn that down?

"Where do you want me?" I asked.

She turned herself around on the sofa so she was lying along it lengthwise. "I'm too boneless to move. Can you make this work?"

Was she inviting me to straddle her and fuck her face?

Oh hell, yes.

"I'd say so, yeah." I climbed over her, with a knee on either side of her body, and crawled up until my groin was level with her mouth. I unzipped my pants, shoved them down, and placed my hands on the arm of the sofa, leaning my weight on them as I angled myself toward her mouth. Fiona's slender fingers encircled my cock and directed it into the wet heat. She sucked, and I groaned in response. She tilted her head and reached around to grip my ass and urge me forward.

"Fuck, Fi." I moaned as she took me deep. "That's so hot."

When she swallowed around my length, her throat milking me, my hips stuttered and I had to struggle not to come. I wanted to enjoy this, not give her the impression I couldn't last long enough to satisfy her. A woman like Fiona had standards, and I'd meet them if it killed me.

I thrust into her gently, keeping my strokes shallow. She sucked, her lips stretched around my cock, and her eyes glazed with lust. She was easily the most enticing view I'd ever seen.

"You take me so beautifully," I praised.

That seemed to encourage her, and it wasn't long before she'd taken me right to the edge. I was shaking, cursing, letting her hear my appreciation. When my balls tightened and tingles started at the base of my spine, I tried to pull back, but she held me in place. Panting, I emptied in her mouth, shuddering as she gently licked my oversensitive cock. Before I collapsed and hurt her, I flopped onto the thin strip of sofa between her and the edge and wrapped my arms around her.

"Thank you," I murmured.

She smiled like a cat with the cream. "I enjoyed it."

"Me too."

She laughed, the sound husky from the way I'd used her throat. "I never saw us ending up here."

I kissed her cheek. "I did, but I wasn't sure how I'd ever get past your dislike of me."

She grimaced. "I'm sorry about that. It wasn't fair of me to think the worst of you just because of how you look. It wasn't intentional, but I should have done better."

I secured her against my chest. "I get it."

I knew how it felt to be betrayed. Perhaps her betrayal hadn't resulted in any physical harm coming to her, but it had still completely upended her life. Some people might say Bergen had destroyed the life she'd built, but I happened to think she'd risen from the ashes pretty damn impressively. I wanted to tell her how much I could sympathize, but that would mean being open about things I'd never talked about. Not even Ronan and Kade knew the full story of how I'd ended my employment with the agency. They knew I wasn't on good terms with my former bosses. I hadn't wanted to relive the trauma I'd been through, and at the time, it hadn't seemed necessary. Now, though? Now, maybe, it was.

If I wanted a real chance with Fiona, I'd have to share my history with her. We couldn't have a relationship built on lies. And yeah, she hadn't said she wanted a relationship with me, but if I wanted that to change, I had to do something about it. She'd trusted me when she jumped off the side of the *Claudette* and plunged into Lake Michigan. In return, she'd discovered that I'd kept things from her. It was time to show her that I trusted her in return.

"Hey, Fi?"

"Mm?" She turned to me sleepily, but something in my expression must have startled her because she frowned and tried to sit up straight. We shuffled around together until we were side by side on the sofa. "What is it?"

I hesitated. "There's something I'd like to share with you, but you can't ever repeat it to anyone else. Not even your closest friends. If you'd rather, I can keep it to myself, but you're the first person I've ever wanted to tell."

18

FIONA

I gazed at Zeke, feeling the weight of his question. When he'd set out to distract me, I'd never have guessed that we'd end up here. I liked it, though—his willingness to trust me. It made me feel as though I wasn't alone in the fondness I was developing for him, and while I desperately wanted to know what secrets he was keeping, I also didn't want him to feel pressured or as if I prioritized my own curiosity over his needs.

"If you want to tell me, I'd be honored to listen," I said. "Nothing you say now will ever be repeated to anyone else. I promise."

His eyes softened. "I trust you." He kissed my forehead and his chest expanded as he inhaled deeply. "You asked once about where I worked before I started King's Security with Ronan and Kade."

"I did."

"I was employed by a government agency right out of college. This particular agency is always on the lookout for young recruits with useful skill sets, and because of my specialization—I won't bore you with the details—and my position on the college gymnastics team, they offered me a job."

"You were a college gymnast?" Perhaps that wasn't the detail I ought to have focused on but it had certainly come out of left field.

He grinned. "What? You can't picture me on the high bar?"

I shook my head. He was fit, there was no denying that, but I would have picked him as more of a motocross rider than a gymnast. "So, what happened after they hired you?"

He looked up at the ceiling. "They put me through all kinds of training, and then I started assignments. At first, I was primarily in the office, handling logistics and the cyber side of things, but I gradually began to work in the field too. My last mission... it didn't end well."

His body was tense, and I smoothed my hand over his chest. He was still looking at the ceiling. Maybe that made it easier for him to speak. I got the feeling he rarely opened up to anyone about anything, let alone this.

"I went undercover in a cyber-terrorist cell with another operative, Ernesto. For the first few weeks, it was fine, but then Ernesto began behaving strangely. I didn't mention it to our boss. Being undercover can do things to a person, and I thought he was just having a hard time."

"But?" I asked warily.

He sighed. "Ernesto had turned. He set me up and made it look like I was the one who'd gone rogue."

I stiffened, my heart going out to him. I understood all too well how that kind of betrayal felt. Especially from someone he'd trusted.

"My own team captured me and brought me in for 'ques-

tioning.' Let me tell you, the agency makes police interrogation tactics seem like a chat with friends."

"But surely you explained?" I asked.

"Ernesto had done an excellent job of making me look
guilty. They assumed I was lying, and they didn't bother
doing a polygraph because we'd all been taught how to beat
them."

I raised an eyebrow. That would be a helpful skill. No
wonder he lied so easily.

"They asked me for answers, and when I couldn't give
them, they tortured me. They thought if they tried hard
enough, they'd break me." His voice was matter-of-fact, but I
flinched.

"They tortured you?" I whispered, my stomach sinking.
"Was it bad?"

"Yeah." He nodded stiffly. "They're really good at making
you want to die without risking it actually happening."

"I'm so sorry." The words couldn't possibly make up for
everything he'd been through, but he deserved to hear
them. I kissed his chest and held him tight, hoping he'd take
comfort from the embrace.

"Thank you." He kissed the top of my head. "Eventually,
the group attacked the water supply system in Washington
D.C. The agency headed it off before too much damage
could be done, but only because a member of the cell had a
crisis of conscience at the last minute." He was quiet for a
moment, then added, "That's also how they found out that
Ernesto had been the turncoat, not me."

I couldn't imagine how that must have gone down.
"What did they do?"

His mouth twitched. "Stopped torturing me."

"But they set you free and issued an apology, right?" In
these times, people couldn't get away with doing that kind of
crap.

He laughed bitterly. "Hardly. I can't be certain, but I think they intended to get rid of me."

My chest seized. "What?"

His fingers tightened reflexively on my shoulder. "By that point, I knew too much, and they couldn't trust that I'd keep the knowledge to myself. Most agents can retire without fear because the agency is sure of their loyalty, but after what they'd done to me, they knew they'd broken any loyalty I had to them."

"But they obviously didn't...get rid of you," I whispered, tears prickling my eyes at the mere thought. If that had happened, I wouldn't have met him, and I couldn't imagine my life without him in it—even when I'd just thought of him as the obnoxious guy at work who flirted too much.

"No, they didn't." His voice was strained. "Because I made it clear that I had information that would implicate a few high-ranking officials and could destroy their careers or even get them imprisoned. If anything happened to me, those records would have been sent to the media. So, they let me go, but they didn't want to. The only thing that keeps them from coming after me is mutually assured destruction."

My heart ached at the thought that Zeke still might not be safe, even all these years later. He'd done nothing wrong, and yet he paid a price for someone else's mistake. I could understand now why he held his cards so close to the vest, and used his charisma as a defense mechanism. If I were him, I'm not sure I'd ever trust anyone again.

"It was smart of you to have a contingency plan in place," I told him.

"It would have been smarter for me to report Ernesto's behavior and figure out what he was up to sooner," he said regretfully. "I was lucky I had a fallback plan. I'd done it on the advice of another agent, but I'd thought I was being paranoid. I never believed I'd actually have to use it. I was so fucking naive."

"I'm sorry." I wished I could make it better for him. I bit my lip when it quivered, so he wouldn't notice, and cuddled closer. I couldn't take away the pain of his past, but I could make sure he didn't regret sharing this with me. "I guess we both have trust issues, although it's fair to say yours are more well-deserved than mine."

He made a sound of disagreement. "It isn't a competition."

"I know."

"But..." he started hesitantly. "I would like to try to work through those trust issues together, if you're up for that."

ZEKE

I HELD MY BREATH WHILE I WAITED FOR HER REPLY. I WAS asking for a lot. My issues ran deep, and I wasn't an easy person to be close to, but I desperately wanted her to agree. If she did, I'd tell her anything she wanted to know about my past. I'd be an open book for her, and I knew she'd be a vault of secrecy in return. But what if I was too much? Too damaged, or broken. Fiona deserved the best, and quite frankly, that wasn't me. But I'd damn well burn the world down for her if she asked me to.

She didn't keep me waiting for long. Her lips curled into a small smile. "I'd like that."

Relief hummed in my veins. She raised herself up and kissed me. This time, it wasn't hungry or demanding, but soft and sweet. It felt like a promise.

I gathered her close and sank into the kiss, wishing it

could go on forever. Right now, with her lithe body pressed against me, I didn't feel so alone. I could imagine a reality in which it wasn't me against the world but *us* against the world. In the past, I'd had teams of skilled operatives at my back, with millions of dollars of resources behind us, but nothing had ever made me feel as supported as she did.

I could fall in love with this woman. If I wasn't already.

She drew back, but I chased her lips. There was nothing sexual about it, I just wanted to hold onto the connection between us for as long as I could. She indulged me, and we kissed slowly until the neediness within me eased enough for me to stop without worrying that she might disappear at any moment.

We lay together for a while until the computer pinged and we could see that Bergen was returning to the same residential address he'd previously visited—presumably, his apartment.

"Thank you for sharing with me," Fiona said after we'd watched the dot for a few minutes. "It means a lot, and I know it can't have been easy."

"It was easier than I expected," I admitted. Revisiting that part of my life was never fun, but telling her hadn't been as difficult as I'd thought it would be. I'd known, in my heart, that she wouldn't think less of me for it.

"You must have done some interesting work for them," she said. "Met some interesting people."

"Yes," I replied, wondering where she was going with this.

I turned to face her. Her eyes were wide with interest.

"Did you ever meet any female spies?"

I chuckled. "We didn't call ourselves spies. We were agents or operatives."

She rolled her eyes. "Fine. Did you ever meet any female agents or operatives, then?"

"Plenty." I grinned at her exasperated expression. "Some worked with me, others worked against me."

"How awesome were they?" She lowered her voice. "I bet they were sexy."

My grin widened. I couldn't tell if she was just fishing for information or if she was trying to work out if I'd ever been involved with a fellow agent, but it was an effective distraction from the grim mood that had fallen, and I was here for it.

"Female operatives come in all shapes and sizes, just like the male ones. Sure, some of them played up their sexuality, but others had impressive intellects, and many looked like everyday people. That's half the job, you know. To blend in with everyone else."

She frowned and waved a hand at me. "But you..."

"I got the tattoos and piercings after I left," I told her. "I knew I was safe, temporarily, but I figured that making myself stand out would be a good way of preventing them from trying to bully me into working for them again. Once they'd decided they couldn't get rid of me, they were reluctant to let me go. Looking the way I do now renders me far less valuable as an undercover asset." Besides the whole fact that they'd hardly be able to trust me to go undercover without defecting even if they did pressure me into it. They knew a losing cause when they saw one, but the extra encouragement sure didn't hurt.

"Do you actually like them?" she asked.

"I do." I touched the place where the piercing through my eyebrow would usually be. "I'd always wanted a tattoo but hadn't gotten one because of work."

"I'm glad." She kissed me chastely. "I hate the thought of you doing something you didn't like just to protect yourself."

I resisted the urge to point out that that had basically been my life for years.

"Besides," she added, "they're sexy as hell."

"Yeah?"

"Definitely." A wicked smile curved her lips, but then a shadow passed over her eyes and the smile faded.

"What is it?" I asked, hating the bleakness of her expression.

She rubbed her lips together. "What do you think will happen?" she asked, blinking rapidly. "If I go to prison, I mean. Will I be okay? I'm not as strong as I pretend to be."

Oh, Fi.

I tucked her face against my chest. "We won't have to find out," I said. "Because it isn't going to happen."

Whatever I had to do to ensure that, I would.

Whatever it took.

19

———

FIONA

REVISITING THE WINDY CITY GALLERY MADE ME FEEL LIKE A naughty child. I hadn't broken any laws, and nobody had told me not to be here, but I still felt squirmy as Zeke and I asked the desk clerk to see if Patience was available. Perhaps it was because my old friend had made it clear she wasn't comfortable with my presence the other day, or maybe it was just the fact that being at the scene of the crime wasn't a good look. Whatever the case, my nerves were frayed.

Zeke put his hand on the small of my back and moved closer. "Are you sure you want to do this?"

I'd suggested telling Patience that we had a lead because it might give her peace of mind. She may not have been particularly welcoming toward me, but she didn't deserve to get fired like I had been from my job at the Black Swan Gallery. Especially not when we were so close to tracking down the Monet. Zeke had agreed with my plan, although he'd warned me that if Patience said anything about talking to the police, all bets were off. He was probably only going along with it because it was a good distraction and I'd been going stir-crazy wanting to jump into action, but there were hours left until we'd be able to do that.

This time, Patience's expression when she entered the room was even warier than before. Her gaze quickly took in how close Zeke stood to me and it shuttered even further. I winced, recalling the fact that she'd slipped him her card. He hadn't called, and his current position hinted at how intimate we'd become. Probably not the wisest move. If Patience felt slighted, she was less likely to be open to hearing what we had to say. Oh well, we were doing her a favor by giving her a heads-up. If she didn't want to listen, that was her choice.

"What are you doing here?" she asked coolly.

I exchanged a glance with Zeke, who arched a brow as if asking whether I really wanted to go through with this. I swallowed my hurt and tried not to take it personally. No doubt she was having a difficult time, and wasn't at her best. If I thought about how I'd felt when I realized that Bergen had been able to steal from my boss because of me, I could sympathize. The situation wasn't quite the same, but it was close enough. Someone had stolen from the gallery and her neck was on the line because of it.

"Can we speak in private?" I asked.

She headed toward the wall furthest from the ticket desk, where no one else should be able to overhear. "Is this okay? The gallery owner is here, and I'd rather him not see you in my office when the police have already told us they're looking into you in connection with the theft."

I winced. "This is fine." I drew in a breath, buoyed by Zeke's strong presence beside me. "We think we might know where the painting is. I just wanted to let you know. Hopefully this whole situation will be resolved soon."

Interest flared in her eyes. "You do? Where is it? Who has it?"

Zeke pressed softly against my back, silently reminding me of my promise not to share any details.

"I can't say yet," I replied apologetically. "We need to confirm the details first, and as soon as we do, we'll pass the information on to the police."

She stiffened. "They don't know?"

"No," Zeke answered for me. "There's no point wasting their time if it doesn't pan out."

She nodded as if this explanation made sense. I searched her face. I'd expected that she'd be relieved by our news, or maybe even grateful. Instead, her expression hadn't changed. Perhaps she was skeptical. It made sense that she might not believe us since she still seemed suspicious of me. We'd just have to make her happy to be proven wrong.

"Anyway, that's all we came to say." I tried to smile, but it fell flat. "We'll get going now."

"Okay." She didn't ask any more questions or even seem that intrigued by what we'd told her. I couldn't help but feel let down by her response.

We said goodbye and left. Zeke didn't say much during the drive back to the safe house, and nor did I, despite the fact that our driver worked for King's Security, so we didn't have to worry about him overhearing our conversation. Zeke had his phone out, presumably to keep an eye on Bergen's movements. Meanwhile, I was mulling over our conversation with Patience. Something about the encounter had been off, but I couldn't put my finger on what.

The driver pulled up outside the apartment block and let us out. Before we could make it as far as the door, Detectives Harrison and Goodwin intercepted us. Goodwin's hand was on his holster, and Harrison looked primed for a fight. My heart leaped.

"How did they find us?" I murmured to Zeke.

"I don't know." His mouth hardly moved as he spoke. "But I don't like it."

"Miss Ryan." Detective Goodwin came to a stop in front of us. "Please come with us for questioning."

"Why?" I demanded, so shocked by their presence that my filter vanished.

"New information has come to light."

"You can talk here," Zeke said firmly.

Goodwin ignored him. "You can come easily, and have a nice conversation with us, or you can resist, in which case I'm authorized to cuff you and bring you in. The end result is the same. Which would you prefer?"

My gut bottomed out, and my eyes grew hot. I was so tired of being treated like a criminal. "I'll come with you, but I won't speak without my attorney."

I nodded to Zeke, indicating for him to contact Ariadne. When he returned the nod, I knew he'd understood. I went onto my toes and kissed him.

"You don't have to go," he murmured.

"It's just easier." I'd fought them before, and it hadn't worked out well for me. Once I was in their interview room, they had no legal way to make me talk. If I kept my temper in check and my tongue in my mouth, I'd get through it.

"Okay." He gave my hand a brief squeeze. "Be careful."

"I will."

I allowed myself to be bundled into the back of their police car. I remained quiet on the drive to the police department. When I was ushered into an interrogation room, I expected questions, but instead, Harrison dropped a manila folder on the desk in front of me.

"Open it," she ordered.

I considered refusing but curiosity got the better of me. Inside were two things: a photograph of me standing beside

Claudette Laurent, and two smudgy fingerprints side by side.

"Explain to me," Harrison said, "why you were seen with a suspected dealer of stolen art, and why your fingerprint was found inside the Windy City Gallery."

ZEKE

I couldn't believe the police had come for Fiona again. Was the fact they'd turned up immediately after we visited the gallery a coincidence or had Patience called them?

I shook my head. No, if Patience had called them, they wouldn't have been fast enough to tail us back, let alone beat us there. How had they known we were here?

Unless, of course, their own cyber team had been searching out the King's Security safe houses. I'd done a good job of hiding any trails connecting them back to the company, but a seriously skilled specialist would be able to uncover them.

I called Fiona's attorney first. She'd given me the woman's number in case anything like this happened.

"Ariadne," she answered briskly.

"Hi, Ariadne, this is Zeke Watts from King's Security. There's been a development with Fiona." I ran her through what had happened, and she promised she'd head straight to the police station. As soon as she hung up, I called Ronan.

"They've taken her in again?" he demanded. "Did you go with her?"

"Yes, and no, but I intend to go down there as soon as I'm off the phone with you."

"Good." He sounded as frustrated as I felt. "Did they give any indication of why they'd come or how they found you?"

"Unfortunately not."

"Damn."

"You said it." I paused. "Anything you want me to do while I'm there?"

"Just get her out of there. She doesn't deserve this bullshit."

"I know." I wished I could hug her. I knew she was scared about what might happen if we didn't find the Monet, and we were so close to clearing her name. "We'll sort it out."

An hour later, I was pacing the police station's reception area, waiting for any sign of Fiona or Ariadne. The attorney had beaten me here, so I hadn't had the chance to debrief with her, and I had no idea what was going on in whichever interview room they were holding Fiona in. There was nothing I could do right now to get her out, and I hated feeling useless.

"Hey, Tattoos?"

I glanced at the female officer behind the desk, who'd directed the words at me. "What?"

"You mind sitting?" She pointed toward one of the seats. "You're making people nervous."

I grimaced and looked around. Indeed, several others in the room seemed uncomfortable. One guy looked away. Another met my stare head-on, and challenging. A girl in a short dress was wide-eyed and edging away from me. Sighing, I flopped onto a chair.

"Thank you," the officer said.

I grabbed my phone out of my pocket and checked Bergen's location. He was at the residential address and hadn't moved all day. I scanned through my messages, hoping there might be an update from Ronan, but I was out of luck.

Finally, there was movement down the corridor and Fiona appeared. I shot to my feet. Even from a distance, I could tell she was upset. Her cheeks were washed out and her shoulders were slumped. Beside her, Ariadne marched like a warrior emerging successfully from battle. Her chin was up, her back straight, and she strode purposefully toward me. Fiona kept pace with her even though Ariadne was moving much more quickly simply by virtue of her long legs.

I hurried to meet them, and pulled Fiona into my arms. She exhaled in a shudder and buried her face in my shoulder.

"Are you okay?" I asked.

"I will be." She sounded tired. "I'm just so sick of this. I didn't do it, but they've got a photo that Bergen must have taken on the yacht, and apparently, they found my finger-prints in the gallery."

I drew back and noticed the two detectives not far behind them. "Let's talk more elsewhere." I put an arm around her waist. "Come on, beautiful."

Ariadne fell into step beside us. "No charges have been pressed. If they hassle you at all, I want to know immediate-ly," she told us. "If they had enough evidence, they'd have arrested you. They're just hoping you'll crack if they press hard enough."

We exited the building, into the gray light of the after-noon. I blinked as my eyes adjusted, and noticed Fiona doing the same.

"Do you need to speak to Fiona?" I asked Ariadne.

"Not unless Fiona has something specific she'd like to talk about." She directed the comment to Fiona, who shook her head.

"I'll review their evidence so far and see if I can poke any holes in it," Ariadne said. "But until they press charges, I won't make anything official. Unless you'd like to sue for harassment?"

"No."

I was surprised by how quickly Fiona replied.

"They have their reasons for suspecting me," she said. "I don't like it, and I think they're being narrow-minded, but I can understand why they're pursuing me as a suspect."

Ariadne snorted. "Be petty, woman. It's far more fun."

Fiona gave a small smile. "Maybe next time." She turned to me. "Is there a car here for us?"

I nodded. "I drove." I took the keys from my pocket. "Come on."

We farewelled Ariadne, and once we were in the privacy of the car, I leaned over and kissed Fiona.

"I'm sorry this is happening," I told her.

She sighed. "It is what it is."

Concern pricked my heart. Where was her usual fiery spirit? I didn't like seeing her defeated.

"Can you tell me everything that happened after they picked you up?" I asked.

She ran me through the conversation, including the temper Ariadne had been in when she arrived. I smiled at the thought. Even if Fiona hadn't given them hell, at least someone had. When we reached the office, I parked in the basement and we took the elevator up. Once again, Kade and Ronan were already waiting for us in Ronan's office.

I tipped my chin to them in acknowledgment. "We have to stop meeting like this."

20

FIONA

"Have a seat," Ronan said.

I sank onto a chair, wishing he had a sofa or armchair I could collapse into instead. I was mentally exhausted. The police had flung questions at me about the photograph of myself with Claudette Laurent and the fingerprint of mine they'd found within the Windy City Gallery. They wouldn't say which room they'd found it in or when, so I couldn't be sure if it was a print I'd left behind after our visit on Saturday or if Bergen had somehow planted one. I didn't imagine that would be easy to do, but he was clever and creative. If anyone could pull it off, he could.

"Are you okay?" Kade asked, his expression sympathetic.

"I just want this to be over," I replied.

"We'll do our best to make that happen soon," Ronan said.

Zeke pulled his chair closer to mine and draped his arm over my shoulders. I appreciated the comfort, although I didn't love the raised eyebrows from my boss.

"King and I have been strategizing," Kade said. "We think Zeke and I should be the ones to check out the commercial storefront that Cole visited yesterday. We'll have a backup team positioned around the corner. I've already chosen a location. They can't get too close or they might draw too much attention, but they should be close enough to assist if we run into trouble."

"Wait." I forced myself to straighten despite my weariness. "Haven't you considered that if you go in without me, you run the same risk as on the yacht? If the painting is there, you won't be able to tell if it's the original or a forgery."

Kade and Ronan exchanged glances.

"We can take a photograph," Kade said. "We're just scouting it out at this point. We're not going to snatch it."

"A photograph may not be enough for me to make a judgment call from." I wasn't trying to be difficult, but I doubted they planned to turn on any lights while they were in there, and a photo illuminated by a flashlight beam might not be very helpful. If they were using night vision goggles and no flashlight, the quality of a photograph could be even worse. "I need to see it in person."

"I'll go in with Fi," Zeke said, his fingertips brushing my shoulder. "We'll be in and out in a few minutes. Purely reconnaissance. Right, Fi?" He gave me a look that said agreeing with him was the only way I'd get anywhere near that painting.

"Right," I said. "I won't try anything. I don't want to cause problems; I just want to be sure."

Plus my stomach fizzed at the idea of setting my eyes on a Monet that I hadn't seen before. They didn't need to know that though.

Kade looked uncertain. He turned to Ronan. "What do you think?"

Ronan shrugged. "You're the expert. I'll support whatever you think is best."

Kade's dark eyes studied me. It felt as if he was trying to look into my soul. I bit my lip, nerves rolling through me. Eventually, he nodded.

"Okay," he said. "But if you're inside for longer than ten minutes, we're coming in for retrieval. Agreed?"

"Agreed," Zeke replied.

I nodded. "Yes."

That was more than fair. I was well aware I was pushing my luck by insisting on being part of the operation. I just couldn't stand being sidelined and having to hope that nothing went wrong. This way, I could actively influence the outcome.

"As soon as we confirm whether or not *Daisies* is being stored at the site, we'll get the hell out of there," Zeke said. "We'll retreat to a safe distance and make a call to the police with an anonymous eyewitness account. Whether or not they believe it, they'll have to follow up."

Relief flowed through me at the thought that tonight I might be able to sleep in my own bed again, with no fear of being thrown in a holding cell. I had no desire to ever spend time in one of those again. I was too soft.

"It's still a few hours until dark," Ronan said. "Why don't you sort out clothes and equipment, touch base with the backup team, and see if any of your people have found anything useful, Zeke?"

"Sounds good." Zeke rose from the chair and offered me his hand. I took it, my cheeks flushing.

Ronan waved a hand between us. "Is this something we need to talk about?"

I snuck a look at Zeke, unsure what he thought. We'd agreed to try to work through our issues together, and I wanted to continue being able to kiss him and luxuriate in the sensation of being held by him, but we hadn't agreed to a label, so I couldn't be sure what he had in mind.

"Fiona and I are seeing each other," he said, sending me a soft smile that hit me right in the feels. I smiled back, a little giddy. "We'll fill out whatever paperwork we need to make it above board with the company as soon as this is over."

"Good." Ronan cleared his throat as we continued to gaze into each other's eyes. "That's all I ask." His tone softened. "I'm happy for you both."

"Thanks." My face heated, and I finally tore my gaze from Zeke's. He threaded his fingers through mine and tugged on my hand. Together, we left the room.

Zeke checked in with various people. I listened and didn't interrupt. There hadn't been any new developments from his team, and Kade's backup team seemed to be on top of the situation. A few of them smiled at me and wished us the best. Even though I didn't know them well, they seemed genuine, and their care warmed me.

Finally, it was time to prepare.

"So, do I get to wear a cool super-spy outfit?" I asked as he led me toward the supply room. He laughed. When I asked why, he didn't reply.

Ten minutes later, I had my answer. Apparently, my badass ninja outfit consisted of black yoga pants and a loose black hoodie. I scowled at myself in the mirror. So much for looking tough. I was more likely to be mistaken for a mom on the way to pick up my kid from school. At least the bulletproof vest he'd given me to wear beneath the hoodie added something to the look.

Arms settled around my waist and lips brushed the side of my neck. *Zeke.* I melted against him as his tattooed fingers interlaced over my abdomen. I loved having him this close. It had been so long since I'd allowed myself to indulge in intimacy with a man, and that it was Zeke, who—far from being the carefree guy I'd assumed him to be—had proved himself to be caring, honest, and worthy of my trust... it meant everything.

"Are you sure you want to do this?" he murmured near my ear.

ZEKE

I WAITED FOR HER RESPONSE WITH BATED BREATH. I HOPED SHE didn't think I'd asked the question because I thought she was weak or I didn't trust her. I just wanted her to know that she didn't have to. It would be more difficult, but we could do this without putting her in danger.

She pulled free of my hold and turned, resting her hands on my waist. "I need the closure. Wouldn't you have wanted the chance to prove Ernesto guilty personally, and make him pay for what happened to you?"

"Yes." I understood exactly what she meant. Even after the agency realized I wasn't the traitor, I'd had a burning need to get revenge on Ernesto. I'd trusted him, and he'd betrayed me. I'd been tortured, partially drowned, beaten, deprived of food and water, and mentally scarred because of him. "I actually did go looking for him as soon as I'd healed enough," I admitted. "But the agency had already gotten to him, and there was no trace of him anywhere. I think they did to him what they'd intended to do to me."

My gut curdled at just how close to death I'd been.

"So, you get it." She waited for me to nod. "I need to be there."

"Then that's what we'll do." I hadn't expected her to

change her mind, but at least I'd given her the option. Honestly, I respected her for knowing what she needed and for making it happen. Too many people didn't have that level of self-awareness.

I cupped her face and kissed her softly. "You're incredible."

Her eyes skittered away from mine, and I frowned. Fiona always projected the image of self-confidence, but I was beginning to think a lot of that was a facade. The same way my persona had kept me safe, her prickly aloofness toward people she considered threats had protected her.

"I mean it," I insisted. "Whatever happens tonight, and whatever comes of this, I want you to know that I won't let you take the fall for something you didn't do. Do you believe me?"

She gazed into my eyes, and it struck me for the first time how similar the color of hers were to mine. We were different in a lot of ways, but the deep, dark brown of our eyes matched almost perfectly.

"I believe you mean that," she said after a moment. "But I don't see how you can keep your promise."

"Just trust that I will." I'd do whatever it took. Kill whoever needed to be killed. Blackmail anyone that needed to be blackmailed. Fiona wouldn't end up in prison. Although I couldn't guarantee what my own future might look like. People in positions of power didn't tend to take kindly to my tactics. The agency had left me alone so far, but if I created other enemies, I'd have to watch my back.

"I trust you," she whispered.

My heart full, I captured her lips. Silently, I vowed that she wouldn't regret her decision.

She stepped closer and tilted her head. I touched my tongue to hers and groaned at how goddamn good it felt. Her body pressed to mine and I skimmed my hands over the slight curve of her hips and around to her ass. She let out a breathy whimper, and my cock hardened. She rocked against me.

"Damn, woman," I panted. "If you keep that up, we're going to make a mess in here."

She smiled mischievously. "I want to."

I hoisted her into the air, my hands cupping her ass as she wrapped her legs around my waist. I backed her against the wall and trailed my lips up the side of her neck, nipping at her earlobe. She shivered.

"Hey, guys? Oh, shit." The door, which had opened without us noticing, slammed shut.

I groaned and lowered Fiona to the ground, holding on to her for long enough to make sure her legs wouldn't give out beneath her. "Was that Kade?"

Fiona's face was bright red. "I think so."

I smoothed her hair down and tidied my clothes, which were rumpled from her body and hands. "Come on. We'd better go see what he wants."

As we exited the room, Kade turned toward us with his hands over his eyes.

"My eyes are scarred," he teased. "I might never see again."

Fiona swatted his shoulder. "Like you and Sage are any better."

He colored and dropped his hands from his face. He seemed to want to protest, but he couldn't when Fiona had spoken the truth.

"What do you need?" I asked, taking pity on him.

"The team is ready to go," Kade said gruffly. "Are you two all set?"

I nodded. "Heading out now?"

"Two minutes."

We assembled in the basement parking area. Kade's

backup squad had already prepared a vehicle. Fiona and I would be taking one of the sedans we used for undercover assignments. It was white, mid-range, and looked unremarkable, but it had been fitted out with top-quality technology and a speed booster. Hopefully, we wouldn't need to make use of that.

Fiona became more and more quiet as we loaded into the cars and followed Kade's team out of the building. They'd be getting into place before we went in, to make sure we were covered. I didn't push her to talk, sensing that she needed the silence to work through something. I glanced at her a few times, noting her pale face and clenched fists, and considered reminding her that she could pull out if she wanted, but I doubted she'd appreciate my interference.

We pulled onto the side of the road while Kade's team parked near a disused service station, and waited until Kade gave us the okay to move in. I checked to make sure Fiona had her night vision visor ready to go. We wouldn't wear them until we were inside, in case there were security lights on the exterior. Thankfully, the dim light cast by the streetlights would be enough to get us where we needed to go.

I tensed as we traveled the last few hundred yards, then I shut off the engine and switched off the lights. Before either of us got out of the car, I reached over and took her hand.

"Just so you know," I said quietly, "I've never had a better partner in crime than you."

21

———

FIONA

MY HEART GAVE A SQUEEZE. I COULD SEE IN ZEKE'S EYES THAT he meant every word. I opened my mouth to respond, but before I could make a sound, he'd slid out of the car and put distance between us. Perhaps it was just as well. He had communications set up with Kade and his team via a recording device in his watch, so they could probably hear us. Now wasn't the moment to confess the emotions building within me. I could do that later, in the privacy of my apartment.

I got out, closed the door quietly, and hurried after him, carrying the night vision visor. Thankfully, my shoes made little sound on the concrete as we rounded the building. I'd been worried there might be dogs, but Zeke and Kade had assured me that few people used dogs for security anymore, and the electronic jammer tucked into Zeke's shirt would interfere with any external electronic security system that Bergen had in place. Zeke's team had tried to figure out what system he was using, but without getting eyes on it, it

174

was impossible to be certain. Whatever the case, Kade would give us a heads-up if anyone came in our direction.

Zeke took a set of lock picks from his pocket and got to work on the lock. The faint scratching sounds seemed amplified in the darkness. I shifted restlessly. It felt like he was taking forever. I didn't dare tell him to hurry up though, in case my voice caught the attention of anyone in the area. Finally, something clicked, and he pushed the door open.

Inside, a keypad glowed yellow on the wall. He attached a small device to it and we both held our breaths, aware that at any second, either a silent or audible alarm might go off. If the Monet was being kept here, I *really* didn't want to be caught with it. I counted in my head. When I got to three, the lights behind the keypad vanished and we both exhaled with relief.

"Visor on," Zeke murmured. "Gloves too."

I slipped it over my head and watched as the room came into focus, then pulled a pair of latex gloves from my pocket and pulled them on. We were in a back foyer. A door to the left opened onto an unclean bathroom, with what looked to be mold in patches on the floor and walls. To the right was a small room that might once have been an office, but was now littered with used syringes and God knew what else. I wrinkled my nose in disgust.

My heart hammering, I followed Zeke forward, where the small foyer opened into a wider space with a counter in front of one wall and shattered glass cabinets that used to house cigarettes. In here, the floor was clear. Someone had recently tidied up. In the center of the room stood two objects covered by a light sheet. My breath caught. *Two* paintings?

I moved toward them, but Zeke put a hand on my arm to stop me.

"Slowly and carefully," he said quietly.

We eased toward the objects. Once they were within reach, we took a corner of the sheet and lifted it off to uncover what lay beneath. My hand flew to my mouth. It was *Daisies*. Or rather, two versions of it. Thank God. Part of me had worried we might be on a wild goose chase. I scanned the paintings. Were they both copies or was one of them the real deal?

Zeke nudged me with his shoulder, and when I turned to him, he cocked his head in question. I held up a finger to indicate to him that I needed a minute. I studied them both. The workmanship was exquisite. It was almost impossible to tell them apart, and they both looked like they could be the right vintage. But then I spotted something that gave it away. One of those brush strokes I recognized as Bergen's signature style. It was nearly invisible, just a tiny flick in the bottom right corner, but it was there.

I released my breath and pointed. "That one is a copy. The other..." I returned my attention to the second painting. The use of layers and the play of light were unparalleled. While the forger had done a remarkable job of mimicking it, nothing could rival an original. "This is it," I whispered in awe. I reached out, wishing I could touch the painting, but if I did, I might leave a trace of myself behind. The gloves weren't foolproof.

Behind us, someone clapped.

I jolted in surprise. Light exploded across my vision, blinding me. I tore the night vision visor off and spun around. White spots danced in front of my eyes. I could hardly see anything. Slowly, my vision cleared. Beside me, I sensed Zeke stiffen as he realized the same thing I had. Bergen was here, and he was aiming a gun directly at me. But he wasn't alone. At his side stood... I blinked, wondering if my eyes were deceiving me.

"Patience?" I asked.

The other woman sneered. Her hair was tied back, her face devoid of makeup, and her outfit was similar to mine, except for one very significant difference: the gun that hung loosely from her hand.

"What's going on?" I demanded, my brain struggling to process this turn of events. "Why are you here?"

Bergen laughed. "Poor Fiona. Didn't see that one coming, did you?"

I shook my head. "I don't understand."

Something solid brushed my arm and I realized that Zeke had closed the space between us. He had a weapon of his own, but I doubted he'd risk going for it when both of them were armed and focused on us.

"We were played," Zeke said. "They're working together."

My stomach sank. Now that he'd said it, it was obvious. Bergen and Patience were here together, and Patience didn't seem to be under any duress. She was part of this, maybe even from the beginning. Fury and hurt coiled and burned inside me. She'd helped set me up, or at least gone along with it, which meant she most likely knew I hadn't been involved with the original theft. I couldn't believe she'd do this to me. Perhaps we were no longer friends, but I hadn't thought she hated me, and surely that's what it would take for her to betray me like this.

I looked at Patience. At the grim set of her mouth and the tightness of her shoulders. "Why?"

ZEKE

· · ·

Hot anger had swamped my body. My fingernails bit into my palms as I stared at the duo in front of us, wondering whether I'd be able to get my weapon out before they could react. I was fast, but it had been a long time since I'd been tested in a situation like this.

Damn, why hadn't I put the pieces together before now? I'd considered the inside man angle, but I'd given it up too quickly when none of the suspects seemed a likely fit. Patience had a clean record and no debt, but that didn't mean she didn't have expensive aspirations or bad taste in men. Now, because of my oversight, we'd been blindsided, and Fiona was experiencing a second betrayal. I had no doubt how much this must hurt her.

My watch vibrated once on my wrist, probably to let me know that Kade and his team were listening. I couldn't communicate with them directly without cluing in Bergen to the fact that we weren't alone, so I dropped my hand and tapped out a code on the side of my leg, telling them to wait for further instructions. If they burst in here right now, they'd easily take Bergen and Patience down, but someone might be hurt in the process—someone like Fiona. I didn't want to risk it. Especially not if there was a way I could work their appearance to our advantage.

As soon as I finished tapping, I edged my hands together in front of me, slowly enough not to alarm them. I made a show of interlocking my fingers, then deftly slipped one of my thumbs around to tap the button that would record any audio being transmitted from here back to Kade.

"You want to know why?" Patience asked, speaking for the first time.

"Yes. I don't understand," Fiona said.

Bergen's expression was gloating, but he remained silent and allowed his partner to respond.

Patience smiled. "Love."

Fiona looked stunned. "What?"

Patience laughed. "Well, that, and money."

She exchanged a glance with Bergen that spoke volumes.

"They're fucking," I said crudely.

"We're in *love*," Patience snapped. "We've been together for years."

"Years?" Fiona's tone was strained, but I kept my gaze on our enemies instead of checking on her, waiting for a moment of weakness.

"Who do you think gave him an alibi four years ago?" she asked, her voice full of glee. "It was perfect. We made you out to be a jealous ex-girlfriend who was trying to pin her crime on poor, innocent Bergen, and everyone believed it."

"You were together then?" Fiona no longer sounded crushed. Just defeated.

"We were, and you never noticed." Bergen tsked. "You really are so naive. Sneaking around behind your back was almost too easy."

I made sure my watch was positioned in the best place to record their words. They hadn't actually confessed to either crime yet, but hopefully they would soon.

"When they didn't charge you with anything the first time around, we were worried," Bergen continued. "But after a while, we realized it was a blessing. It meant we could use you as a patsy again, but this time, we wanted to make sure it was worthwhile. Selling a Monet will set us up for life."

"So, you admit you stole it?" I prompted, for the benefit of the recording.

Bergen rolled his eyes. "What does it look like?"

Damn, that wasn't confirmation.

"So, what's the plan here?" I asked. "Why the extra forgery? You already used one as a decoy for the theft."

This time, it was Patience who replied. "The other forgery wasn't intended to do more than delay the discovery of the theft. We wanted people to notice, and to blame Fiona. We worked on this forgery together for months. We started as soon as we found out that *Daisies* would be coming to the gallery. The copy is perfect. If we call in an anonymous tip and Fiona is found with it in her possession, she'll be arrested and everyone will believe the original painting has been returned to its owner. There will be no need for anyone to look deeper. Meanwhile, we'll sell off the original and start a new life somewhere tropical and without an extradition treaty."

Perfect. That was exactly the confession we needed.

"What will you do when Bergen double-crosses you?" Fiona asked.

"He won't." Patience sounded smug. "You were a means to an end for him. I'm his soul mate."

I watched for Bergen's reaction. A twitch of his mouth gave him away. I knew beyond a doubt that if it came down to him or Patience, he'd drop her so fast she'd get ground shock.

Fiona laughed bitterly. "You think you have it all worked out, but you're forgetting something. I'm not the only one here. Zeke won't let you pin the theft on me."

A sliver of warmth unfurled within me at the certainty in her voice.

Bergen's smirk widened into a lopsided grin. "You're forgetting something, darling. Dead men don't talk."

My watch vibrated again. Our conversation must be making Kade nervous. I took a moment to evaluate whether Bergen would shoot me here and now. The Monet and its copy were uncovered behind me. Surely he wouldn't risk damaging them. I tapped out another message for him to wait.

"You can't do that!" Fiona cried. She moved in front of me, putting herself between us. My heart ka-thunked. What a sweet, beautiful fool. I wouldn't let her risk herself for me. "People will notice if Zeke disappears. People know we're here."

Bergen just shrugged. "It's a dangerous neighborhood. He was mugged, and it went wrong."

She scoffed. "No one will believe that."

I couldn't help grimacing. There were enough people who wanted me gone that, if not for Kade and his team listening in, they probably would be able to sweep it under the rug. I nudged Fiona to the side and took her hand.

"Just breathe," I murmured. "I'm going to get us out of this. Trust me."

Bergen must have heard me because he barked a laugh. He raised the gun and pointed it at my head. "I'm afraid that's a promise you won't be able to keep."

22

———

FIONA

Zeke kept his eyes on me. They gleamed in a way that made me nervous. Was he going to do something crazy?

"Trust me," he whispered.

"I do."

He pressed a button on his watch. The movement was obvious. None of us missed it.

"What did you do?" Bergen demanded.

Zeke grinned at him. "Wouldn't you like to know?"

Bergen rushed over to us, grabbed Zeke's arm, and looked at the face of his watch. I knew what he'd be seeing. No matter what parts of the technology were active, the front screen only ever displayed the time and a step count for the day. Zeke had designed it that way for exactly this reason, and every King's Security employee wore one when they were in the field. My guess was that he'd pushed the button to summon Kade and his team to get us out of here. The only question was, why now as opposed to five minutes ago? And why had he been so obvious about it?

"Take it off," Bergen ordered, pressing the muzzle of his gun against Zeke's head. Zeke calmly removed the watch. Bergen snatched it off him, dropped it on the ground, and crunched it beneath his heel. It wouldn't matter. If Zeke had sent out an alert, Kade's team would be bursting through the doors at any minute.

"He could be psyching you out," Patience said, but she sounded shaken.

"Or he could have sent for help." Bergen circled Zeke, grabbed the gun hidden beneath his jacket, and slid it to Patience. "We can't risk it. We have to get out of here."

"Let's take him with us," Patience suggested. "We can use him as a hostage and negotiate to make sure no one gets in the way of the police arresting Fiona."

Bergen grinned. "I love the way you think, darling."

"No!" I cried out. I couldn't let them take him, or he was as good as dead.

"Fi." Zeke's voice was soft. "It's okay."

I frowned, my emotions spinning out of control. "Don't you dare sacrifice yourself for me."

He mouthed, "Trust me."

I wanted to fight. To scream and shout and throw punches at the people who'd made my life hell and were now trying to take away the one good thing that had come of it. I couldn't lose the man I was falling for. I couldn't. But he was asking me to trust him. Maybe he had a plan. He held my gaze, and I gave a slight nod.

He returned a small smile, and his mouth formed silent words. I couldn't be certain, but it looked a lot like, "I love you."

"I love you too," I whispered back, the words coming easier than I ever would have imagined.

"So tragic." Bergen shoved Zeke, and he stumbled.

"You're going to walk out the back exit and to the left. Don't make a fuss or I'll put a bullet in your head."

I swallowed a whimper as Zeke walked away with Bergen behind him. He didn't even look over his shoulder.

"Patience, get the painting," Bergen called.

Patience skirted around me, giving me a wide berth, and hefted the Monet. I considered charging at her, but she still held the gun with one hand, even if it wasn't aimed at me, and anyway, if I did, it might throw off Zeke's plan, so I let it happen. Everything in me screamed to do *something*, and I had to remind myself that I was.

I was trusting Zeke.

A moment later, Patience was gone, and the door shut behind her. I waited, hoping to hear the sound of a confrontation. Surely our backup couldn't be far away. I raced to the door and pulled it, but it was locked. I searched for a mechanism to unlock it, but there was nothing. The door must only lock from the outside.

I ran to the other door, which used to be the shop entrance, but it was boarded up. I pried at the wood with my fingers, but it didn't budge.

"Fuck," I breathed.

The windows were boarded up too. Hold on a second. The ones out the front were, but what about the ones in the back?

Outside, I heard raised voices, the squeal of rubber on concrete, and a gunshot. Then there was a thud, another shot, and silence. My heart skipped. What had happened? Had someone been shot?

I raced into the bathroom, choosing not to look at my surroundings, and tried the latch on the window. It didn't open, so I scanned the room, spotting a piece of timber leaning against the wall in the corner. I grabbed the board, weighed it in my hands, and then lined it up with the window. I swung it like a baseball bat, but the glass didn't shatter. I stared in disbelief. Only the tiniest chip had appeared. It must be reinforced. I swung again, aiming for the chip, and again. Gradually, a crack appeared, and then the glass panel crumpled outward. A moment later, a face wearing a visor appeared in the window.

"You okay?" Kade asked.

***

ZEKE

I WENT WILLINGLY AS BERGEN COLE PUSHED ME INTO THE vehicle he'd parked around the side of the building. I hadn't seen it earlier because we'd approached from the other direction. We should have cleared the area first, but I wasn't expecting him to be here, so I hadn't bothered. That had been an oversight. Clearly, after we'd spoken with Patience about our lead, she must have gone straight to him and they'd decided to use our plan to their advantage and sat in wait for us.

That's what we got for trusting someone.

And yet, Fiona trusted me. I wouldn't let her down. I smiled to myself. Maybe it made me certifiable to find joy in a moment such as this, but knowing she trusted me to protect her meant everything.

Patience came racing out of the building, carrying the Monet. Bergen popped the trunk open and she slid it inside, then slammed the trunk shut and got into the front passenger side. I flopped against the back seat, keeping low in case Kade's team arrived and started shooting. They were trained to use non-lethal means of apprehending people if possible because it was easier to keep the police happy that way, but they'd shoot if they had to, and this might be a situation that called for it.

The car lurched forward. Outside, I saw a flicker of movement, and then a figure appeared in front of us. A muzzle flashed and the windscreen shattered as a bullet tore through it. Glass tinkled to the floor. I rolled toward the side door and tried the handle, but it was locked. I flicked the lock and tried again, but it didn't budge. I cursed. He must have used his override button to shut down all the locks in the car.

Another shot cracked in the night, and Bergen cried out as it punctured his shoulder. He put his foot on the accelerator and the car rocked, an awful thud sounding as we hit a person. My gut tightened. I hoped whoever it was would be okay.

I lurched forward, reaching for Bergen's weapon, but I found myself staring down the barrel of Patience's handgun.

"Don't fucking move," she hissed. Her eyes were wild, and I stopped, knowing she'd shoot me in an instant if she thought she had to. "Put your wrists together. Slowly."

Bergen didn't slow the car as we hurtled around a corner. I wondered if anyone from King's Security was on our tail. I had another tracker in my shoe that I'd worn in case anything happened to the watch, so they wouldn't have any problem following us.

Patience pulled a zip tie from her pocket and glanced from it to my wrists. Realization seemed to dawn on both of us at the same time. She couldn't put it on me without lowering the gun, and I could hardly zip-tie my own wrists.

I smirked. "What's your plan with that?"

She dropped it and moved so quickly I wasn't prepared when the gun smashed into the side of my head. My vision went hazy and then dipped out.

When I opened my eyes again, my head was throbbing

painfully and my wrists were bound together in front of me. Damn, she must have knocked me out and taken care of it while I was unconscious. At least my legs were still free.

In the front, Patience was on the phone, speaking with a phony British accent.

"Yes, that's right," she was saying.

I rolled my eyes, then winced in discomfort. The accent was clearly fake, and whoever she was talking to must know it.

"She had red hair, and she was tall and slim. She had something with her." A slight hesitation, and then she added, "A painting, maybe. It was hard to tell in the dark."

It must be the police.

"Help!" I yelled, knowing it would take a few vital seconds before Patience or Bergen could react, during which time the officer on the phone might hear everything. "I've been kidnapped!"

Patience ended the call and whipped around. She aimed the gun at me. Honestly, with how much time I'd spent staring down the barrel of a gun tonight, it was starting to lose its sharp edge of fear.

"Can I shoot him?" she asked Bergen.

"Not here." He sounded as if he found the idea distasteful. "Too much cleanup. We'll drop him in a quiet alley somewhere. That way the mugging story will be an easier sell."

I snorted, despite the pain beating through my mind. "You must know that no one will believe it. Come on. My company is investigating you and the next minute Fiona is in jail and I'm dead? The police aren't stupid."

"We don't need them to be," Bergen replied. He shifted in his seat and I heard his quick intake of breath. The gunshot wound must be bothering him. How much blood had he lost? Enough to pass out? One-on-one odds were better than two-on-one, even if Patience was armed and I wasn't. "As soon as we've sold the Monet, I can pay off whoever the hell I need to to make it stick."

"Good plan. Real solid. That's definitely not going to land you behind bars."

"It will work." His tone was grim.

"It will," I agreed. "You'll be in prison in no time, and I'll be free to kiss the hell out of my woman. I appreciate you making it so easy."

Bergen glanced over his wounded shoulder. "What the hell is your deal? Do you want to die?"

No.

I'd never had a death wish, and I'd done things I wasn't proud of to save myself in the past, but I'd never wanted to live quite this badly before. Fiona gave me a reason to want to stick around and find out what the future held. When I did leave this world, it sure as hell wasn't going to be because of an asshole like this guy.

He pulled over and shut off the engine. I raised up enough to peer through the windows. We were in a dark alley, exactly as he'd said. There was a click as he unlocked the doors.

"Get out," he ordered.

23

FIONA

I COULD HAVE KISSED KADE, I WAS SO GRATEFUL TO SEE HIM.

"I'm fine," I said. "But they have Zeke."

"Shit." He drew back and tapped his earpiece. "The suspects have Zeke. Approach with caution." He was quiet for a moment as someone replied to him, then said, "Follow them. The tracker will lead us straight to them. Don't shoot again unless there's no other option. We don't want Zeke caught in the crossfire. Understood?" Another silence, and then he turned to me. "They've escaped in a vehicle. The driver may have been shot, and one of our men was injured by the car. We're on their tail. We'll get Zeke back."

I clutched my chest. "They got away?"

Why had I let Zeke go with them? I should have fought. I'd failed him.

"Not for long," he assured me. "Can you let me into the building?"

"It locks from the outside."

"Right." He nodded. "We'll try to pick the lock, and if that fails, we'll come in by force. We'll get you out of there, Fi."

"Don't worry about me." My throat was thick with emotion. "Just save Zeke."

His mouth formed a line. "Zeke's top priority is making sure you're safe. He made me promise that I'd stay with you personally if anything were to go wrong."

A sob escaped me, and I clapped my hand to my mouth. That damn fool had put me before himself once again. Didn't he realize that he was important too?

"Wait there and don't move," Kade said, vanishing from view.

My stomach churned as I stared into the dark. My eyes adjusted, and I could see figures moving, some coming closer and others leaving—hopefully to go after Zeke. I couldn't believe this had gone so wrong. It was supposed to be a simple reconnaissance mission. But because I'd wanted to take the pressure off Patience and let her know we were on our way to a breakthrough, everything had gone pear-shaped.

This was all my fault.

There was an almighty crash and the sound of splintering wood. I rushed out of the bathroom and gaped at the ragged hole where the door used to be. Somehow, it had been torn off its hinges, and it had taken a chunk of the doorframe with it. The whole thing lay at my feet. Kade dropped something that looked like a battering ram, stepped through the doorway, and scanned me from head to toe, perhaps confirming that I was unharmed. He removed the night vision visor and squinted past me into the shop area.

"Is that the painting?" he asked.

"No, it's a copy. They took the real thing with them."

He rubbed his jaw. "We'll leave it. Let's get out of here."

He offered me his hand, and I reached toward him, but we both froze when a siren wailed in the night. Blue and red lights filled the alley behind us, and the King's Security team hurried to holster their weapons.

I closed my eyes and groaned. As if this wasn't bad enough, the cops were here.

"Come on." Kade put an arm around my shoulders and guided me out. "We'll sort this out."

I wasn't so certain.

"Fiona Ryan." I winced at the familiar sound of Detective Harrison's voice. "What the hell is going on?"

"We confronted the thieves who stole the Monet from the Windy City Gallery," Kade said as the pair of detectives approached. "They escaped in a dark sedan with a hostage."

Goodwin arched his eyebrow. "You expect us to believe that when it looks like you're up to no good and just trying to cover your tracks?" He glanced past us and stilled. His eyes widened. "That's it." A grin spread over his face. "That's the Monet. Halle-fucking-lujah."

Harrison brushed past us and went to the painting. She scanned it and pulled a phone from her pocket, possibly checking it against a photo of the original.

"It looks like it," she agreed, and unhooked a pair of handcuffs from her belt. "Hands out, Ryan."

My jaw dropped. "Are you serious?"

For God's sake. They were letting Bergen and Patience get further away. They needed to get a move on, and call for reinforcements.

"That's a forgery!" I exclaimed. "Any impressionist art expert worth their salt would be able to tell you that if you give them a few minutes to study it."

Yes, perhaps they wouldn't be able to identify Bergen's

signature brush stroke the way I had, but they'd still be able to prove it was a fake.

"In that case, you're in possession of a forgery," Harrison said. "Either way, you're coming with us." She jerked her head at Kade as she clamped the cuffs around my wrists. "You, too. As far as I'm concerned, you're all accessories to a crime. We just need to work out exactly what the crime is."

My jaw clenched. "While you're working that out, they're getting away with the real Monet. Zeke is in danger. Please. I don't care what you think you know. Please help him."

Harrison looked at Goodwin, who shrugged.

"Put Officers Smith and Hernandez on the case," he said. "Rather waste their time than ours."

Harrison stepped aside and made a call. Meanwhile, Goodwin gestured at the exit.

"Please, walk ahead of me, Miss Ryan," he said. "Mr. Campbell, do I need to cuff you, or will you come willingly?"

"I'll come," Kade said. "But you're making a mistake."

Goodwin laughed. "That's what they all say."

He opened the back door of the police cruiser and indicated for us to get in. I climbed in and scooted over, making room for Kade.

"I'm so sorry about this," I murmured. Our current predicament was all on me. If I hadn't dated a thieving asshole four years ago, none of this would ever have happened. Zeke wouldn't be in harm's way and Kade wouldn't be in a tight spot with me.

"It's not your fault," he said, as if reading my mind. "We chose to be involved. The only person to blame for this is Bergen."

"And Patience," I added, still shocked by the second betrayal. Somehow, even though we were no longer friends, I felt blindsided by her actions. Back when she and Bergen had supposedly started sleeping together, we *had* been friends. What kind of person screwed their friend's boyfriend?

Harrison emerged from the building and got into the passenger seat just as Goodwin claimed the driver's seat.

"Backup is two minutes out," Harrison said. "They'll secure the scene and start questioning witnesses."

"Great." Goodwin eased the car forward, moving slowly. He didn't pull out of the property until another police car—lights flashing—swerved in beside us. Then he raised a hand to the other cops and started the journey back to the police station.

"Please make sure someone is looking for Zeke," I pleaded, not afraid to beg if it meant he came home safely. I was terrified of what they might do to him, especially if he antagonized them.

When we reached the police station, they separated me from Kade. I was escorted to the same interrogation room they'd put me in last time. I expected them to start asking questions, but instead, they left immediately. The lock clicked ominously into place behind them.

ZEKE

"I'd rather not," I told Bergen, knowing that as soon as I got out of the car, they'd probably shoot me.

"Get out," he repeated, waving the gun in my face. His complexion was waxy, his jaw tight with pain.

"No, thanks." I didn't move an inch. "I have absolutely no incentive to get out. If I do, you'll shoot me. You apparently don't want to make a mess in your car, so I'm safer if I stay right here."

"Patience." He shot his girlfriend a look. "Get him out."

Wide-eyed, Patience got out of the passenger door and moved around to open my door. Bergen climbed out of the driver's seat, reset the locks, and joined her. The way he was holding his shoulder made me think he'd need to seek medical treatment soon. He was an artist. He wasn't used to dealing with this level of pain. Adrenaline was keeping him going for the moment, but it wouldn't for much longer.

Patience cautiously bent and reached for my ankles to drag me out. I snapped one of my legs up, kicking her in the face. She reeled backward, blood spurting from her nose.

At that moment, another vehicle pulled up behind us and men spilled from it, rushing at us. Bergen spun, raising his gun with his good arm, but he was too slow. Someone tackled him to the ground, disarming him in the process. Patience flailed, still bleeding, as a dark figure leaped on her and pinned her arms behind her back. A silent struggle ensued, and a minute later, both Bergen and Patience were subdued, their hands cuffed and an armed guard standing over them.

"Zeke, you all good in there?" I recognized the voice as belonging to David, one of Kade's unit leaders.

"Peachy," I called. "Great timing."

David appeared in front of me and helped me up. "Your tracker made it easy."

He unsheathed a knife from his belt and cut the zip tie off. I rubbed my wrists. They tingled as blood flowed back into my hands.

"Is Fiona safe?" I asked, cutting straight to the chase.

"Hold on." He grabbed his radio. "Let me check in. We switched communication channels after we separated from the others, so we couldn't get our wires crossed." He turned away and spoke to someone at the other end. When he turned back, his expression had darkened. "She's safe."

"Thank fuck." I allowed myself to feel a sliver of relief, but not too much. His expression made me wary. "But?"

"Apparently a couple of detectives turned up shortly after us. They took Fiona and Kade in for questioning, and according to Vic, it didn't look friendly."

My hands tightened into fists. "Those fuckers."

As if Fiona hadn't already been through enough. They must have gotten there so quickly because of the call Patience made. I'd hoped my interruption would cast doubt on their story, but it seemed it hadn't been enough.

"Did anyone find my watch?" I asked.

David repeated the question into the radio. "They've got it, but it's damaged," he said.

I forced myself to draw in a slow breath. It wouldn't do anyone any good if I self-combusted. "Someone needs to check whether the recording device is still functional, and if so, take a copy and get it to the police immediately. I used it to record our confrontation."

A grin spread across David's face. "Good thinking. I'll get them on it immediately."

"Can you take me there?" I asked. "Actually, wait. Have the watch sent to Jonah in the office and tell him it's urgent. I need to get to Fiona ASAP."

David's smile faded. "About that..."

My eyes narrowed. I didn't like his tone. "What about it?"

He held his hands up in a gesture of peace. "I'm just the messenger." He shifted from one foot to the other. "We have orders from Ronan not to let you talk to the police without him there. Something about damage control. He also wants you to be checked over by a medic."

I growled, frustration building within me. I felt jittery after my narrow escape, and however well-intentioned it might be, I wasn't in the mood for Ronan's meddling. "Have him meet us there," I said. "With a medic too, if he insists.

And tell him we're bringing these two." I waved at Patience and Bergen. "Cole will definitely need a medic, but I don't want him out of our sight."

David studied me for a moment, then nodded. "That should work. I'll talk to Ronan. What should we do with the painting?"

I hesitated. "Call Joanna Lee and ask her to come, or to send a cop she trusts. I know it's not her department, but insist. Tell her I'm collecting on a favor."

"Got it."

"Also, don't leave the painting alone. I want at least two people guarding it at all times until the police have taken it in as evidence. They'll be able to confirm it's the real deal."

He jerked his chin in acknowledgment and barked orders into his radio. A few minutes later, we were crawling toward the police station at exactly a mile an hour less than the speed limit because David refused to run the risk of getting pulled over when we had handcuffed criminals in the back seat. One of his team rode in the back with them to keep them in line, while David and I sat in the front. When we finally arrived, I threw the door open before we'd fully stopped and rushed toward the entrance. Ronan was there with Jared, one of the medics we called in when needed.

"Hey." To my surprise, Ronan stepped forward and hugged me. "I'm glad you're okay."

"Me too. Thought I wasn't going to be for a minute there." I glanced toward the entrance. "Fiona is still inside?"

He nodded. "Are Cole and the gallery manager in the car?"

"Yeah."

His jaw tightened. "I'll make sure they're dealt with appropriately."

He clapped me on the shoulder and strode off, leaving

me with Jared. The medic was on the shorter side, with a slim build and sandy blond hair.

He gave me a friendly smile. "Do you have any injuries other than the bruising on your face?"

I tried to remember whether I'd been hurt anywhere else, impatient to get inside. "I don't think so."

There hadn't been much in the way of a struggle since I'd gone with them willingly in a bid to get them away from Fiona.

Jared studied my face. He grabbed my chin and tilted my head one way then the other before prodding my tender cheekbone. I bared my teeth but didn't wince.

"I don't think there's anything broken," he said and fished a flashlight from his pocket. He aimed it into my eyes. "Pupil movement is even. What day is it?"

"Tuesday, or maybe Wednesday at this point."

He ran me through a few more questions before he seemed satisfied.

"I don't believe you're concussed, but just to be safe, have someone stay with you overnight and try not to sleep for more than an hour or two at a time."

I nodded, familiar with the spiel. This wasn't my first head knock.

"You should ice your cheek," he said, although his expression told me he knew I didn't intend to bother. He waved a hand. "Get going. Go find out how your girlfriend is."

"Thanks, Jared." I left before he changed his mind and made a beeline for the reception desk inside the station. A young man sat behind the glass partition. His eyes widened as I approached.

"How can I help you?" he asked, his tone surprisingly firm.

"I'm here to see Fiona Ryan."

I was getting her out of here ASAP. I just hoped someone had called Ariadne.

The guy typed something into the computer and frowned. "I'm afraid you can't see Miss Ryan yet," he said apologetically.

I scowled. "Where is she?"

24

FIONA

My voice was hoarse. When Harrison and Goodwin first left me in here, I'd shouted through the door, hoping to get their attention or at least force someone to listen to me. Perhaps yelling hadn't been the best way to go about it because now my throat hurt and the few people I'd seen had given me some serious side-eye.

Now I heard the lock unsnick and a uniformed officer poked their face in and then stepped aside to allow Ariadne to enter.

"Thank God you're here," I exclaimed. "Do you know if Zeke is okay? No one will tell me anything."

She smiled tightly. "The good news is that he's fine. King's Security caught up to them and were able to apprehend your ex and the gallery manager. Zeke is a little bruised, but he's more worried about you than himself." Her smile turned wry. "He created quite a scene out there, demanding you be set free. They had to have him removed from the building."

I hardly heard the second half of what she said, too relieved by the first half. "Thank you." A knot inside me loosened, and it felt like I could finally breathe again. "How badly is he hurt?"

"Just a black eye and a swollen cheekbone," she said. "I think he was pistol-whipped."

I winced, but considering I'd been fearing the worst, I was only too happy to kiss his bruises better later. As long as he was alive, and his usual cocky self, everything else would be all right.

"Did they arrest Bergen and Patience?" I asked.

She sat opposite me at the table. "The detectives on the case are questioning Patience at the moment." She pursed her lips, looking hesitant.

"What is it?" I asked.

She sighed, pulled a pen from her blazer pocket, and spun it between her fingers. "The police are reluctant to press charges against them because even though they were allegedly found in possession of a Monet, they were apprehended by King's Security, so the police don't have any proof of what went down. The chain of custody is a mess. There are witnesses who will swear that Patience and Bergen had the painting, and Zeke is prepared to testify that they kidnapped him—the recording of the call Patience made to the police should help with that since you can hear him in the background—but it's going to take a while for them to sort through everything and figure out a way forward."

I blanched. "Excuse me?"

On some level, I understood. The police hadn't seen Bergen with the Monet personally, but how much evidence did they really need?

Ariadne's expression was sympathetic. "I'm sorry, Fiona. It might be a while before you're officially cleared."

"But surely they can connect the abandoned shop back to Bergen, and that's where the police sighted the forgery."

She nodded in acknowledgment. "Hopefully, but as I said, it might take a while, and your presence there muddies the waters."

"What about the existence of the second forgery?" I asked. "Surely that makes them suspicious."

"They'll look into it. They just might not be as fast as you'd like." She grimaced. "They have to do everything by the book, and they can't move as quickly as private companies can. There isn't much we can do to change that."

My shoulders slumped. I might not like it, but she was right.

"There is one other thing that might help you," she said tentatively.

I cocked my head. "What?"

"Zeke recorded your conversation in the abandoned shop using the device on his watch. The police have the watch and the recording. King's Security made a copy before they handed it over, and I've listened to it." She hesitated, then added, "It's pretty damning."

I straightened. "They have a recording?" I tried to remember exactly what had been said. I had a feeling that Patience had basically given a full confession. "Doesn't that solve everything?"

Ariadne huffed. "I wish. Unfortunately for you, audio recordings in Illinois require permission from both parties or they're unlawful. Taking that into account, and the fact that voice identification hasn't been run yet, they're not officially recognizing the recording as evidence."

What the hell? Zeke had dropped gift-wrapped evidence of my innocence onto their laps but they'd decided to ignore it?

"Hopefully, even if it isn't officially recognized, they'll

still take it into account during their decision-making." Ariadne sounded more optimistic than I felt.

"Is there anything we can do at the moment?" I asked.

"You just need to sit tight and not say anything without me present." She placed her hands on the table and leaned forward. "I'm sorry, I know that's not what you want to hear, but it's just the way it is. I'll see if there's any way I can get you out of here faster, but they're allowed to hold you for forty-eight hours."

Yeah, I knew that. Ariadne and I had had this same conversation four years ago. Back then, I'd been younger and confused. At least now I knew what I was up against.

"Thank you, Ari."

"I've got your back, girl." She stood and brushed her suit down. "Take care of yourself, and don't speak a word."

"I won't."

She gave me a hug and left. The lock clicked into place once again. I wondered whether an officer was standing by the door in case I tried to make a run for it. I imagined myself shoulder-charging the door, then sprinting for the exit, only to be mowed down by a burly cop. No, thanks.

I paced the length of the room, wishing I knew the time, but they'd taken my phone and my watch off me, and there was no clock on the wall. Hours seemed to crawl by. I had no idea how long it had really been, but at some point, an officer brought me a sandwich. They returned a while later and walked me to the bathroom. I ate again—perhaps lunch —growing increasingly desperate to hear what was going on.

Then the worst happened. The officer cuffed me and escorted me to the holding cells.

"You'll be in here overnight," she said, waiting for the guard to open the cell door.

I stared straight ahead, feeling like I might cry. I didn't

belong here. Although, to be fair, the girl in the corner didn't look like she did either. She wasn't more than a teenager, wearing a short skirt and too much makeup. Her eyes were frighteningly vacant. A big, olive-skinned woman eyed me like I was fresh meat, and I gulped. She could snap me like a twig if she wanted.

"In you go," the officer said, giving me a little push.

I stepped inside the cell, terror brewing in my gut. A Black lady sat against the wall, watching me curiously. She looked the most composed of my new companions, so I edged toward her, putting more distance between myself and the others.

Please get me out of here.

ZEKE

IT WAS ALMOST MIDNIGHT BY THE TIME THE POLICE DECIDED to release Fiona. If not for my pushing, they'd probably have left her in their holding cells until the morning, but I remembered how much she'd said she hated her time in the cells four years ago, and I was determined that she wouldn't spend a second longer in them than necessary.

The police's crime scene team had pulled together enough evidence to charge Bergen and Patience with the theft. Video evidence showed Bergen spending far more time at the storefront than Fiona had, and both his and Patience's fingerprints were on the painting. They'd been so confident they wouldn't be caught that they hadn't bothered to wear gloves.

Amateurs.

The police had also found a collection of close-up

photographs of *Daisies* hidden in a file on Bergen's laptop. Apparently, when he and Patience had discovered it would be coming to the Windy City Gallery, he'd flown to Paris to view it in the Louvre and had taken photographs and notes to recreate it as closely as possible. There were a bunch of other threads that had come together, but suffice it to say, the police had finally realized that Fiona had nothing to do with the theft.

I waited for Detective Harrison to join me near the entrance to the holding cells. She and Goodwin were doing overtime so they could get the painting back to its very wealthy owner as soon as possible. She scowled at me as she approached, her nose crinkled like she'd smelled something bad. Perhaps her boss had chewed her out for the mess she and Goodwin had made of this case. If she'd listened to Fiona and at least looked into Bergen to begin with, maybe everything would have been worked out much sooner.

"Come on," she said gruffly.

I followed her past the guard, who handed her a key, and into the cells. I immediately spotted Fiona sitting beside a slim Black woman, her knees pulled up to her chest and her eyes bloodshot. She looked exhausted, and she'd probably been too anxious to get any sleep. She turned toward us slowly, then blinked, as if coming back to herself. She stood on shaky legs and came over, reaching for me between the bars.

"I'm so glad you're okay," she whispered. "I was so scared when you let them take you." She scanned my face, her gaze darkening as it lingered on the bruising on the side of my cheek.

"I'm fine, and you are too," I told her. "We're getting you out of here."

"Really?" Relief soaked her tone. She turned to Harrison. "I'm leaving?"

Harrison opened the door and ushered Fiona through, then shut it again rapidly. I hauled her into my arms. She relaxed into my embrace, letting the tension drain out of her body. Her mouth found mine and we kissed, slow and thorough. One of the women in the cell catcalled.

"Cut it out," Harrison said.

Fiona drew back, her eyes never leaving mine. "Don't ever do that again."

I frowned. "What do you mean?"

"Use yourself as a distraction," she said. "You mean too much to me to risk like that. Your safety is just as important as mine."

I wisely kept my mouth shut, even though I disagreed. I'd give everything to keep her safe, and I'd never have a moment's regret for doing so.

"Okay, lover boy, get a move on," Harrison urged.

Fiona's nostrils flared, and she looked like she wanted to hit someone—preferably Detective Harrison—but she stalked out of the room. I matched her stride for stride, and footsteps behind us indicated that Harrison was keeping pace too. When we reached the elevator, Fiona turned to face Harrison.

"Can I leave?" she asked.

Harrison nodded. "No charges are being filed against you. You're free to go, although we may want to speak with you more as a witness."

Fiona's eyes narrowed. "Give me at least twenty-four hours to recover, and don't bother asking me to come in without my lawyer."

Harrison rolled her eyes but didn't comment.

"And?" I prompted the detective.

Harrison glared at me, and then turned to Fiona. "The department apologizes for any distress you may have experienced as a result of our investigation both now and in the past."

"Thank you," Fiona said.

While it was obvious Harrison hadn't wanted to say it, she had, and apparently Fiona was going to take that as a win. Considering she'd lost her job four years ago, she'd be within her rights to sue, but Harrison hadn't been the detective involved with that case, and honestly, I thought everything had worked out for the best. Well, everything except the fact that Fiona had stopped making art. She had a gift, and it was sad to know she'd cast it aside because of a cheating asshole who'd never deserved her in the first place.

Harrison handed Fiona her phone and her purse, then I took Fiona's hand and we left the building together. As we stepped outside, she stopped walking and pulled me closer. She gazed up at me with dark, soulful eyes, and the edges of her mouth lifted.

"Thank you for getting me out of there," she said. "And..." She nibbled on her lower lip. "I'm not sure exactly what's happening between us, or where we go from here, but I want you to know that I love you." She released a puff of breath. "It's completely crazy, but I do. I love you, Ezekiel Watts."

I gathered her in my arms and breathed her in, squeezing my eyes shut against the waves of emotion crashing through me. I'd known I was falling for Fiona, but it wasn't until she was out of my reach that I realized I'd already fallen for her. *Caput*. I was done.

"I love you too," I murmured against her hair.

"Yeah?" She pulled back and dabbed at her damp eyes.

"Yeah." I smiled and kissed her. "I'm crazy about every sassy, strong, unbreakable piece of you."

Her expression softened. "What about the broken bits?"

"Oh, Fi." I cupped her face. "Don't you know? They're my favorite."

She blinked rapidly. "You asshole. Now I'm going to cry."

Grinning, I kissed her. Once. Twice. Again. Peppering her beautiful face until she laughed and pushed at my chest.

"Where to now?" I asked. "Want me to take you home?"

"I'd really like that." She hesitated, then added, "Will you stay with me?"

"Always."

25

FIONA

I BURIED MY FACE AGAINST ZEKE'S STRONG CHEST, MY OWN full of mushy emotions that I hadn't experienced... well, ever. I simultaneously wanted to protect Zeke from everything while also curling into the fetal position and letting him take on the world for me. I wasn't sure what to make of it, but I knew that I never wanted it to end.

Zeke took my hand and led me to his car—the silver hatchback that I hadn't thought was a good fit for him. Maybe I'd been wrong. I'd believed I knew all sorts of things about Zeke, but in reality, I'd had no idea who he truly was. I did now.

He helped me into the passenger seat and drove us to my apartment building. I had to admit, while I was grateful to be going home, I was a little disappointed not to finally see his place. We'd learned so much about each other over the past few days, but I still didn't know where he lived. Hopefully, he'd take me there soon. I had a feeling it was his sanctuary.

He parked outside and stayed alert as we took the stairs to my apartment. I unlocked the door and entered hesitantly. It was clear the police had been through. Things weren't where I'd left them, and a few of the kitchen drawers stood open, their contents emptied onto the counter, but on the whole, it wasn't as bad as I'd expected. Zeke's fingers threaded through mine and I held onto him as we checked the other rooms. The bathroom had hardly been disturbed, although my bedroom was another story. My drawers were open and had clearly been rifled through. I shivered. I knew the police were technically the good guys, but I still felt the need to wash everything before I wore it again.

I opened the spare room door last. The paintings that had been resting against the wall were laid out on the ground, facing up. I scanned them one by one, then frowned and counted them. There was one missing. It took only a second for me to realize it was the copy of the Degas. My breath caught. Of course the police had found it. The question was, why hadn't they leaned harder on me because of it? The painting would have given them more ammunition to use against me.

"It was destroyed," Zeke said softly.

I turned to him, surprised. "What was?"

"The painting of the girls dancing." He squeezed my hand reassuringly. "The police never even saw it."

The breath gusted out of me. "Thank you."

"You don't mind?"

"No." I kissed him chastely. "I'm just relieved I don't have to worry about it."

He shrugged. "It was a potential problem, so I took care of it." He grinned roguishly. "That's kind of what I do, Fifi."

I groaned. "Please never call me that again."

"It's cute," he said.

"It makes me sound like a poodle."

He opened his mouth, then closed it. I shot him a look. We both knew he couldn't deny it.

"I need to shower," I said. I hadn't showered for nearly two days now, and during that time, I'd worked up plenty of nervous sweat.

"You do that, and I'll get you a drink," Zeke said. "Wine?"

"Or..." I leaned into his embrace. "You could join me."

He looped his arms around me. "I'm not going to say no to an invitation like that."

"I'm too tired for sex," I warned, not wanting to get his hopes up.

"I know." He didn't seem to care. "I just want to feel you against me, skin to skin."

I swooned a little but tried not to let it show. His ego didn't need any fuel. I returned to the bedroom and took a fluffy robe from the closet. I hung it over the hook on the back of the bathroom door, turned on the shower, and shed my clothes on the tiled floor. Once steam was rising, I stepped under the water and closed my eyes, enjoying the sense of all the grime of the past two days washing off my skin. I heard movement behind me, and a bare chest pressed against my back. Zeke pulled me into the shelter of his body, and I melted against him, finally able to fully relax.

He kissed the side of my neck, spending extra time behind my ear, the tickle of his facial hair making me shiver. He reached for the body wash and pumped it into his hand, then, gently, he started to wash my back. My eyes prickled with emotion as he took his time rubbing the knots between my shoulder blades and tracing the indentations on either side of my spine. Nobody had ever made me feel so beautiful or so cherished.

When he was done with my back, he turned me to face him and kissed me tenderly before repeating the process on my front. He lingered over me as if he was getting as much enjoyment from the simple act of touching me as I was. By the time he finished, I was languid and mellow. I filled my palm with body wash and returned the favor, working my fingers over each of his pecs, the muscles of his abdomen, and his strong shoulders. His gaze was intense as it followed my every movement, but it wasn't sexual. It was as if he simply couldn't bear to look away from me.

We stayed beneath the water until it started to run cold, and then dried ourselves. My limbs were heavy as I donned the robe and we headed to the bedroom.

"Stay?" I asked, repeating my earlier question.

His lips curved. "For as long as you'll have me."

My insides were warm as I removed the robe and got under the covers. Zeke joined me, wrapping himself around me from behind and nuzzling the back of my neck. His hand rested on my stomach and I could hear the soft whisper of his breath. My mind was fuzzy with pleasure, and I was so blissed out from our shower together and from being held in a way I'd only ever dreamed of that I fell asleep quickly.

As I drifted into dreams, I could have sworn I heard him murmur, "I love you, Fiona Ryan."

FIONA

THIS TIME, WHEN I WOKE, ZEKE WAS STILL SPOONING ME. A smile stole across my face. Who would have ever guessed that the badass super-spy was a secret snuggler? I pressed back against him, enjoying the heat of his body and the peaceful rhythm of his breaths. And was that an erection?

"Stop moving," Zeke grumbled. "You're too sexy. My poor cock can only take so much."

My smile widened. Was he utterly ridiculous? Yes. But I loved it.

I wiggled against him slowly and purposefully. "All right, woman," he growled. "You asked for it."

He rolled me over and pinned me beneath him. I beamed up, not in the slightest bit concerned about dealing with whatever consequences he had in mind.

An hour later and freshly showered, we made breakfast together. I'd need to make a run to the shop since I didn't have much here, but at least the coffee was divine. As was the way Zeke smiled across the kitchen counter at me, as if we'd been doing this forever. An ache of longing filled my chest. I wanted that with him so badly. Years of waking up and making sweet morning love, followed by breakfast and tackling the day together. It felt good to have someone on my team. Someone to laugh with, and who I knew would tease me mercilessly when the opportunity arose but would also be my staunchest, most stalwart defender.

"Are you going sappy on me?" he asked, the soft look in his eyes telling me that I wasn't the only one affected by this.

I rolled my eyes but didn't call him out on it.

When we walked into the office soon after, I wasn't surprised by the attention I received. I'd been expecting it. But I hadn't expected the way Stephanie from the front desk ran across the foyer as soon as we left the elevator and hugged me tightly, or the way nearly every person we passed stopped to let me know they were happy for me—or to express outrage and disbelief at what I'd been through. My smile grew steadily as we made our way closer to my desk outside Ronan's office. I'd thought he'd be waiting, so I frowned when I had to knock on his office door.

"Come in!"

I opened the door and peeked in. My jaw dropped. The conference table was covered with food, and people were squeezed into every corner of the room. I spotted Willow and Sage near the front, right before Sage launched herself at me and wrapped me in an embrace. Willow joined her.

"We're so glad you're okay," Sage said.

"Thank you," I choked out, hardly able to speak past the emotion lodged in my throat. My vision blurred as I looked around, seeing Kade standing behind Sage, Ronan near his desk, and each member of the team who'd been our backup squeezed into the space—many of them already munching on snacks.

My gaze fell on Terry, one of the guys on Kade's team. He was leaning against the wall, one arm looped through a crutch, with a moon boot on his foot. "What happened?"

He winced. "I had a disagreement with a car."

I gasped. "I'm so sorry!"

Kade had mentioned someone being hit, but he'd said the injuries were minor, so I hadn't given it much thought.

"It's just a sprain." Terry grinned. "It means I get to sit on my ass for a couple of weeks while it heals."

"Let me know if you need any help."

"I will." He smiled, his teeth white against his darker skin.

"But if you just want someone to play nurse, find your own woman," Zeke warned. "This one is taken."

"Ooh."

I didn't hear who said it, but several faces turned toward Ronan—no doubt to see how he'd react to his assistant dating his business partner.

He sighed. "I'm with an employee myself, so I don't know what kind of reaction you guys expected of me."

There was scattered laughter and the tension lifted.

I did the rounds, talking to each person who'd been kind

enough to be here for me, and exchanging hugs with a few of them. I thanked everyone who'd helped and indulged in a slice of delicious cake that Kade's mom had made. At one point, someone handed me a glass of sparkling wine, and I sipped, enjoying the fizz and tang. Once the office had emptied of everyone other than the directors and their partners, I flopped onto a chair.

"Thank you all," I said. "This was really lovely."

Willow grinned. "It isn't every day you're cleared of being an art thief."

I snorted. "Thank God for that."

If no one ever suspected me of as much as stealing the last pastry in the box ever again, I'd be happy.

"I have something for you." Sage passed me an item wrapped in tissue paper.

I weighed it in my hand. It was heavier than it looked. Carefully, I removed the layers of tissue. Beneath it lay a translucent white crystal shaped and polished to look like a love heart. It was just the right size to sit in the center of my palm.

"It's selenite," Sage explained. "It's a purifying crystal. It'll help you clear out any lingering negative energy."

I smiled. It was just such a *her* gift. "It's perfect."

She sent me a sweet smile.

I cleared my throat. "Thank you all for going to bat for me. You have no idea how much it means to know you were all on my side." I lowered my gaze to my hands so I wouldn't tear up, but the sight of that beautiful clear heart made my lip wobble. "This could have been a total nightmare. I mean, as it was, it wasn't great, but without you, I'd have been lost."

"We're just glad we were able to help," Ronan said gruffly.

"You did more than that." The fact that they'd been there

with me through thick and thin meant more than words could say.

I felt an arm loop around me and I turned into Zeke's embrace.

Kade chuckled. "I have to say, I never thought I'd see the day that happened."

I laughed, the heaviness I'd felt dissipating. "Me neither." I pressed a kiss to Zeke's cheek. "I was blind about what was right in front of me."

"But now you see what a catch I am?" Zeke teased.

I pulled away and smoothed my hair into place. "Sure. Keep telling yourself that."

Then I wandered through the office door over to my desk, from where I had a clear line of sight to the others. I sat and switched on my computer.

"Fiona." Ronan's tone was wary. "You know we don't expect you to work today, right?"

"I want to." Being back here felt right. As if everything was finally right with the universe again. The phone rang, and I picked it up. "King's Security. This is Fiona."

26

———

ZEKE

At the end of the week, I met Fiona at her desk as she was finishing for the day and greeted her with a kiss on the cheek.

"I've got a surprise for you," I announced.

She glanced at my crotch and smirked. "Hardly a surprise."

I put my hand to my chest, affecting a wounded expression. "I'm hurt. I'm not just a one-trick pony. Although, it's a good trick, right?"

"It's a fabulous trick." Her smile became mischievous. "Best trick I've ever seen."

"And it'll stay that way." I wasn't afraid to indulge my possessive side when it came to Fiona. It was strange, I'd never known how many caveman-like tendencies I had until I kissed her for the first time. Now, I'd cheerfully disappear anyone who had the gall to look at her sideways.

"So, what's the surprise?" she asked, slinging her handbag over her shoulder.

"We're going on a date."

"We are?" Her eyebrow arched. We'd hardly left her apartment over the past few days, except to work. That was in part because we couldn't keep our hands off each other, but it had also given her the chance to recuperate after our run-in with her ex and the subsequent shit show with the police.

"Yes," I confirmed, taking her hand. "I can't let you forget that we are, in fact, dating." I smiled at her as we headed toward the exit together. "As in, you're mine, I'm yours, and I can whisk you away on romantic dates on a whim."

"As long as those romantic dates are romantic by both of our standards," she warned, narrowing her eyes at me.

My lips twitched. "You're so suspicious, honey muffin. I promise you'll like it."

At least, I hoped she would. There was a chance I was overstepping, but if she gave the slightest indication that was the case, I'd back off. All I wanted was for her to be happy. Well, and for her to be with me.

I stopped near the exit and released her hand so I could sift through my bag. I pulled out a pair of yoga pants, a tank top, and an old sweater.

"Change into these," I said, gesturing at the bathrooms to the right of the door.

She frowned. "You want me to wear this on a date?"

"Yeah." I nodded, giving nothing away.

She studied my face for a long moment, then took them and vanished into the bathroom. When she emerged, her dress was folded neatly over her arm and she'd let her hair out, so it now fell loosely around her face. The air punched out of me. God, she was gorgeous. Dressed up or down, smiling or scowling, tired or refreshed, Fiona stole my breath.

"What now?" she asked.

I led her to my car and drove us to a small studio not far from her apartment. She looked around with interest as I escorted her to the entrance. I knocked and waited. The door opened a few seconds later.

"Hello!" A petite blonde beamed at us. She opened the door wider and stepped backward. "Come in. Are you ready to have some fun?"

"Yes," Fiona said hesitantly.

"She doesn't know what we're doing yet," I explained to the blonde, Anna. "It's a surprise."

"Oh! How lovely." If possible, her smile widened as she focused on Fiona. "Your man has booked a romantic couples wine and painting night. I have a lovely bouquet of flowers set up for you to paint, and there's several different wines for you to sample, as well as a charcuterie board to snack on. I usually do a short demonstration at the beginning of the evening, but Zeke assures me you won't need any help from me, so I'll just show you around and get out of your way. You'll have the room to yourselves until eight."

Fiona's eyes widened and she turned to me. "We're painting?"

"If you'd like to." My stomach tightened, and I tried to hide my nerves. "We don't have to if you'd rather not, but you're so talented and it seems such a shame that you don't do something you used to love."

She hesitated, nibbling on her lower lip. For a moment, I thought she might tell me I'd butted into something that was none of my business, but then her expression eased and she gave me a soft smile.

"You're right," she said. "I miss painting, and I shouldn't let Bergen take it away from me."

"You'll give it a go?"

"I will."

My insides settled. I took her hand and we followed

Anna, who'd been watching our exchange with interest, through to the studio. The room had off-white walls and was awash with golden light. A bouquet of lilies stood in the center of the room with two canvases set up a few yards away. Fiona went to stand behind one of them, studying the lilies intently. I joined her, picking up a small wine glass from the edge of my easel and sipping it.

"The food and drinks are over here." Anna gestured to a hand-carved wooden table against one wall. "I'll be through there." She waved toward another door. "I won't come in unless you call for me. If you need anything, just knock."

"Thank you," I told her.

She smiled. "Have fun."

I picked up a paintbrush and scanned the selection of paints. I didn't know much about them, although I'd done enough online research to not make a total ass of myself. I watched Fiona surreptitiously as she did the same and twirled the paintbrush between her fingers. I dabbed mine into the fuchsia pink paint and made a start, hoping it would take the pressure off her. She walked over to the bouquet, circled it, and returned to her canvas. Eventually, she sighed, and turned to me.

"I need a more inspiring subject," she said. "The flowers aren't doing it for me."

Damn. I set my paintbrush down.

"What did you have in mind? Maybe we could use one of the wine bottles?" I suggested.

Her lips curved wickedly. "I was thinking more along the lines of you stripping off those clothes and posing for me."

My jaw dropped. "Nude?"

I almost laughed. I sounded like a scandalized old-fashioned housewife.

"Nude," she confirmed, her eyes sparkling with amusement.

I glanced at the door that Anna had left through. "But…"

"She said she wouldn't come in unless we called her," Fiona reminded me.

So she had. I chuckled. What the hell. Why not?

I kicked off my shoes, shucked off my clothes until I was in my underwear, then cast one last look at the door before peeling them down. "Where do you want me?"

She guided me to stand in front of the bouquet, using her hands to adjust me into position. She stood back to survey me, then shook her head and gripped my hips.

"Turn around," she said. "I want you to look over your shoulder at me and give me that smolder that says you want to take my clothes off. You know the one."

I smirked. I did know the one. I followed her orders and held still while she returned to her canvas.

"Fantastic." She grinned, and my heart kicked in response. "Now, don't move."

That didn't seem like a hard ask, but before long, I discovered that standing in one place and trying to hold the same expression wasn't as easy as it looked.

"I have a whole new respect for models," I grumbled.

She laughed. "It isn't easy. I posed nude for an art class once. I had the worst crick in my neck at the end."

My cock stirred. I really hoped Anna didn't pop in to check on us.

"Do you have any of the paintings from the class?" I asked. I bet she'd make a stunning nude model. She'd put Rose from *Titanic* to shame, that was for sure.

"Nope." She sounded gleeful. "But this one is definitely going on the wall."

"Can I see?"

She pursed her lips and eyed it critically. "In another few minutes."

She got back to work, and I amused myself watching the

play of emotions across her face. She was an open book when she was painting, and I loved that. Finally, she put her paintbrush down.

"You can come over," she said.

I stretched, my muscles creaking, and slowly made my way to her side. As soon as I laid eyes on the painting, I forgot how to breathe. I'd expected it to be decent—I'd seen evidence of what a good artist she was—but she was out of practice, and honestly, I'd thought she might be a little playfully teasing when it came to painting me naked.

Not so.

She'd captured me beautifully. The sunlight played across my skin in the painting, and her use of colors and contrast was exquisite. It was my face that most stunned me though. Everything I felt for her was there for anyone to see. I had no idea how she'd done it, but my love for her practically radiated off the canvas.

"Wow," I breathed.

"It needs a lot more work," she said self-consciously.

I took her by the shoulders and turned her to face me. "It's amazing, Fi."

Her lips curved slightly. "It is kind of great, isn't it?" Her smile widened, and she laughed. "I painted, Zeke. I finally did it." She kissed me. "Thank you for bringing me here. It was...sweet."

A few weeks ago, "sweet" might not have been what I wanted to hear from any woman, but now, I was so glad to see Fiona happy, and the fact that I'd contributed to it was fucking amazing.

I bounced my eyebrows. "Just call me sugar."

FIONA

I was riding high as Zeke drove us home from the studio. My painting would stay there to dry—I'd positioned it facing a wall and suggested Anna may not want to look at it—and we could return to either continue working on it or take it home. Once upon a time, I would have considered it far too raw to be finished, but it was the first full image I'd managed to paint in years. I didn't know whether it was being free of the shackles of my past, or simply Zeke's ability to get me out of my head, but I was reluctant to change a single thing about that painting. It was perfect.

It took me a while to realize that we weren't heading toward my apartment.

"Where are we going?" I asked.

"My place." He glanced at me, uncharacteristically hesitant. "Is that okay?"

My heart soared. "Perfect."

The fact that he trusted me enough to take me to his home felt momentous. I'd never heard him—or anyone else —talk about it. I didn't even know whether he lived in a condo or a house of some kind. My anticipation grew as we left the city center and entered the suburbs. He finally stopped outside a small, tidy wooden home with a pair of cane chairs on the front porch and a flower garden that was beginning to die off before winter.

"Home sweet home," he said, and came around the car to help me out. Not that I needed it, but it was a nice gesture.

I stared at the house, unsure what to make of it. I'd expected him to either have a condo with edgy decor in a cool part of town or perhaps an architecturally designed house with a stylish interior. From the outside, this place looked... homey.

"You have a garden," I said, like an idiot.

He flashed me a grin. "Flowers in the front, vegetables and fruit trees in the back."

My eyes widened. "Really?"

He snagged my hand and led me to the front door. "What? You didn't expect me to have a green thumb?"

"Honestly, no."

He slotted his key into the lock and pushed the door open. We stepped into a short hallway, with a shoe rack to one side. I slid my shoes off and placed them on the rack. Zeke did the same.

"Would you like the grand tour?" he asked.

"Yes, please." I was eager to see more.

"This is the spare bedroom." He opened the door to the left, revealing a small room with a neatly made bed in the center, a bookshelf against one wall, and an array of knick-knacks along the top of the shelf.

"The master bedroom is across the hall."

His own bedroom was nothing like I'd pictured. As in the spare room, there was an overflowing bookshelf covered with a random array of items, a nightstand with a lamp, and pillows piled high on the bed.

The living room also took me by surprise. There was a throw on the sofa, giving it a cozy feel, and a well-used coffee table with a candle placed in its center. The kitchen was clean, with a bowl of fruit on the counter. The whole place felt like a home, and being inside it was like receiving a warm hug.

"I love it," I told Zeke.

He smiled. "I'm glad. I never got to have much of a home when I worked for the agency because I had to move a lot, and I was often undercover. I bought this house as soon as I started working with Ronan. It's my favorite place to be."

Emotion swelled within me. "Thank you for sharing it with me."

He drew me into his arms and kissed me. "Thank you for making me want to."

I buried my face in his chest. This whole situation, while lovely, was getting a little too sappy for either of us.

"How about you show me the bedroom again?" I suggested.

"Absolutely."

We hurried back to the bedroom, shedding our clothes along the way. I draped myself over his pillows and ran my hands over my breasts, toying with my nipples, then dipping lower. His eyes darkened as they tracked my movements. He climbed onto the bed beside me and worked his strong leg between my thighs, the hairs rasping against my sensitive skin. I gasped and arched against him.

He licked his fingers and rubbed them over my pussy, teasing my clit and slipping into my wet heat. My hips rocked instinctively as he petted me, moving slowly as if he had all the time in the world. I rolled my body, thrusting my nipples toward him, hoping he'd get the memo and hurry up, but instead, he stopped touching my pussy and smoothed his palm over my inner thighs. Back and forth, skirting the edge of the burning flesh I so badly wanted him to touch.

I reached for his erection and wrapped my hand around it, loving the way he hardened even further in my grip. I worked my hand along his length and teased him with my thumb, stroking his slit, flicking the piercing, and smoothing the precum over his velvety head.

"You play dirty," he murmured against my lips before capturing them in a filthy kiss full of tongue and panted breaths.

"You haven't seen anything yet."

I straddled him and licked his cock from root to tip, then took it inside my mouth.

"Fuck!" He thrust, lodging himself in my throat. My eyes watered, and the sensation of having the Prince Albert piercing so deep was strange, but I swallowed around him, loving the way he twitched inside my mouth. His hands fisted at his sides and his jaw clenched. Damn, he was sexy.

I pulled back and caught my breath, then set to work driving him as close to the edge as possible without letting him tip over. Every time his breathing became ragged and his hips started to roll helplessly, I stopped.

"Enough teasing," he groaned. "You've had your fun."

"I have," I agreed with a wicked grin. I crawled up his body and rubbed my sex against his cock, pleased when he gripped my hips and forced me to be still. Having this man be so close to losing it because of me was such a power trip.

I encircled his cock with my fingers and positioned it beneath me, then slowly sank onto him. He felt different inside me than anyone else ever had—and not only because of the piercing or because he was bare. Just by being *him*, it was different. Making love with Zeke was the most wonderful and intimate experience of my life.

"That's it, baby," he urged. "Ride me."

I rose up and my head fell back as I dropped onto him again. I cupped my breasts, knowing he loved to see me touch them, and found a rhythm that worked me higher and tighter. I looked down at him, and his near-black eyes stared fiercely into mine. They made me feel sexy. Loved.

Adored.

"I love you," I whispered, dropping my hands from my chest.

He reached for one of them, kissed my fingers, and nipped at the fingertips. "I love you too."

My orgasm washed over me like a wave crashing on the shore, and left me shuddering with the aftershocks. Zeke thrust up into me a couple more times before he came with a growl. I lay against his chest, wishing with my whole heart that I could stay in the moment forever. I'd never felt so utterly happy to exist in the present. But if Zeke was my future, I was sure it wouldn't be the last time I felt that way.

I couldn't wait.

EPILOGUE – TWO YEARS LATER

FIONA

"This is how your first yacht experience should have gone," Zeke said as he hand-fed me a plump green grape.

I bit into it, relishing the pop of tartness followed by the sweet. The sun beamed down on us, and I closed my eyes and soaked it up.

"I happen to think our first yacht experience was quite memorable," I told him. "That said, being able to lounge around without having to jump over the side and swim to safety in the middle of the night definitely has its perks."

He took off the captain's hat we'd bought at a costume store prior to boarding and positioned it against the top of my head. It was nearly two years after that fateful evening on the *Claudette* and Zeke had decided I deserved an afternoon of being wooed on Lake Michigan, just us and the yacht's owner, who was giving us plenty of space. I'd happily gone along with the plan, and I'd added my own little twist, which I'd be surprising him with soon. Zeke had turned out to be quite the romantic. It had taken some getting used to, especially after my rocky history with Bergen, but I loved how special he made me feel. It was hard to believe I'd ever thought he was anything like my ex.

"I think you need more sunscreen," he said gruffly.

I grinned. "You just want an excuse to put your hands on me."

"Guilty."

I sat up and pulled the captain's hat more firmly into place. I was wearing a bikini, and even though I was dry, I wrapped a towel around my waist. "I'll be back in a moment."

"But Fi," he protested. "I wanted you to take clothes off, not put them on."

My smile grew. He had no idea what was coming. Trying to get something past a former spy was a mission, but he'd done so much for me, and it was my turn to surprise him. "Don't worry, I'm not getting dressed. Stay right here."

I made my way into the small cabin, where the yacht's owner sat behind the wheel.

"Is it time?" he asked.

I nodded. "Where are they?"

"In the chiller under the drinks fridge."

"Thanks." I bent and removed the two desserts—chocolate lava cake, because it turned out Zeke was a chocolate fiend—from the chiller and sat them on a silver platter. Carefully, I positioned two champagne flutes beside them and collected the champagne on ice. I slipped one last item into my hand and made my way back out onto the deck.

"What's this?" Zeke asked as I approached.

"Dessert." I placed the platter on the bench.

He winked. "I thought you were dessert."

My heart skipped. All things going according to plan, I would be. "You can have me later."

He leaned over and kissed me. "I'll hold you to that."

I poured champagne into the flutes and raised mine. My heart hammered in my chest, and the item still clasped in my left hand slipped as my palm grew sweaty. I tightened my grip on it.

"I propose a toast," I said.

He cocked his head curiously but raised his own glass too. "What are we toasting to?"

I inhaled slowly and gathered my courage. "Let's toast to a long life, a loving relationship, and a strong marriage."

We clinked glasses before he had time to process my words.

His brow furrowed. "What?"

I put my glass down, my hands trembling, and showed him the ring box. I popped the lid open and offered it to him. "I love you, Zeke. You make me laugh, and smile, and you showed me how to embrace life again. Will you marry me?"

His eyes soft, he gazed at me. "Only if," he reached into the pocket of his board shorts and pulled out a matching box, "you'll marry me too."

My jaw dropped, and I gaped at him. "You what?"

He grinned, his joy infectious. "Yes, I'll marry you. Make me the happiest man and marry me too."

I passed him his ring box and took the other, opening it to gaze in awe at the pale pink diamond nestled inside. The ring was elegant but modern, and very feminine. It was exactly something I would have chosen.

"It's beautiful," I whispered, slowly raising my eyes to his. "You were going to propose today?"

He did that half-smirk thing that drove me crazy, but that I secretly loved. "It seemed only polite to have a ring for you since you planned to give one to me."

I stared. "You knew?"

"Yup."

"But how?"

He mimed zipping his lips. "If I told you, I'd have to kill you."

A laugh burst from me, and I grabbed his face and planted a kiss on him. "Yes, you ridiculous man. I would love to marry you." I slid the ring onto my finger and sighed as the diamond glittered in the sunlight. "I can't believe you knew! I was so sure I'd finally managed to keep something from you."

Amusement gleamed in his eyes. "I always know everything, Fi. But you wouldn't have me any other way."

I sighed and flopped onto the seat beside him. It was true. Zeke Watts would exasperate me until my dying day, and that was exactly how I liked it.

THE END

EXCERPT FROM THE LIAR

JOANNA

I checked my phone, but there was still no reply from West. It was unlike him to go so long without responding. Then again, his shift at Henry's, a bar frequented by Chicago's finest, had begun thirty minutes ago, so it was possible he was busy.

"Everything okay?" Hanson asked from behind his computer. Our desks fronted onto each other, but I hadn't realized he'd been paying me any attention.

"Just waiting for a message," I told him, not keen to disclose that I was hoping to hear from my husband.

Hanson and I were too different to be friends, but we'd always treated each other politely. Something in our interactions had changed since I'd married West. It was as if he approved of me finally behaving like a woman "ought to" by getting a husband.

While he meant well, it made me feel a little icky. There was nothing wrong with being a single career woman.

My phone rang, and I answered without looking, hoping it might be West.

"Lee," the voice on the other end said.

I deflated. It was my boss.

"Yes, sir?"

"I want you and Hanson to report to my office immediately."

"We'll be there in a minute, sir." I ended the call and turned to Hanson. "Thackery wants us in his office."

Hanson grunted, and his bulldog-like face scrunched with displeasure. I got it. We were supposed to be half an hour from the end of our shift. Getting called in to talk to the boss now couldn't be good. Unfortunately, that was just how policing rolled. Criminals didn't wait for the most convenient times to commit crimes.

I stood, pocketed my phone and grabbed a notebook. Hanson shot the notebook a glare. He was a decent cop, but he was part of the old guard and believed that the police wasted too much time writing reports and covering our asses when we should have boots on the ground.

He liked to skirt the rules. I was known for being by-the-book. We weren't exactly a partnership made in heaven.

We strode down the corridor that separated the Homicide Department from Missing Persons. The captain's office was halfway along, on the right. The door was ajar, so I knocked and opened it.

"Sir?"

"Come in."

I entered and stepped aside so Hanson could join me. Captain Thackery didn't motion for us to sit. Instead, he tapped a few keys on the computer before raising his gray-flecked head.

"I need you to report to a crime scene near the lakefront. There's been a woman found murdered in her apartment."

I frowned. "You wouldn't rather Neal take the lead?"

Detective Neal, who would be arriving anytime now to

start his shift, had made it clear he liked taking on the cases in that area, and he could get nasty if other detectives encroached on his territory.

Thackery shook his head. "Neal won't be in tonight. Bad prawns, apparently."

Hanson and I both grimaced. Even though I didn't like Neal, I wouldn't wish a bout of food poisoning on anyone.

"We'll drive over now," I told him. "Who's already at the scene?"

"The medical examiner is on the way, as are a team of crime scene techs. There's a pair of beat cops keeping lookie-loos away until reinforcements arrive."

Hanson and I took our leave. Hanson muttered under his breath as we packed our bags and hastened to the car.

"Deborah will have my head," he said as he climbed behind the wheel—because God forbid he should allow a woman to drive. "She's been cooking all afternoon. She's testing a new recipe."

"She'll understand." After more than thirty years married to a cop, Deborah Hanson undoubtedly understood the demands of the job more than most.

"I'm sure you had plans with your man too," Hanson said, pulling out of the parking garage and onto the street.

"I'm supposed to bring him dinner at Henry's," I admitted, taking my phone out to send West a quick message explaining that I'd be late.

We didn't speak much as Hanson navigated the city streets. That was all right with me. I wasn't much of a talker. We drove past the apartment building that Thackery had directed us to, but there were no parking spots available, so we had to park a block away and walk back.

As we passed a coffee shop, I glanced inside, and my heart nearly stopped.

I jolted to a halt, nearly tripping over my feet.

No.

No, no, no. It couldn't be.

A chill stole over me and my chest squeezed painfully. Seated in a booth at the coffee shop, holding hands with a beautiful blond woman, was my husband.

My stomach lurched. I shut my eyes and opened them again, praying I'd been mistaken and that the man in the coffee shop only resembled West. But no, it was definitely him.

A wave of nausea washed over me, and I clapped my hand to my mouth, unable to tear my gaze from them. The blonde was leaning toward West, her hair spilling over her shoulders, framing cleavage that a Playboy bunny would be proud of. She was all curves and creamy skin, the complete opposite of me with my slim build, dark hair, and olive complexion.

"Why'd you stop?" Hanson asked, jolting me out of my reverie. He followed my gaze through the window, and his eyebrows inched up his forehead. "That's your man, isn't it?"

"Yes. It is." I jerked into motion, forcing my legs to carry me past the coffee shop, toward the crime scene that awaited us.

I couldn't handle it if West saw me here. I needed time to get my thoughts straight before I faced him. A little quiet, so I could piece together what I'd seen.

"Slow down, Lee," Hanson wheezed, struggling to keep up. "Maybe it wasn't how it looked."

"You're probably right." My voice seemed to come from somewhere outside of myself. I felt like I was hovering above my body, watching everything from a distance.

You're detaching, my brain helpfully supplied. It often happens to victims of crime or—

Nope. Not going there.

Perhaps Hanson was right and there was a reasonable explanation. God, I hoped there was. My throat ached and I blinked back tears as we turned into the apartment building. Hanson pressed the button for the elevator.

Don't fall apart now.

ALSO BY A. RIVERS

King's Security

The King

The Veteran

The Spy

The Liar

Crown MMA Romance

Fighter's Heart

Fighter's Best Friend

Fighter's Secret

Fighter's Second Chance

Crown MMA Romance: The Outsiders

Fighter's Frenemy

Fighter's Fake Out

Fighter's Mercy

Fighter's Forever

ACKNOWLEDGMENTS

Thank you, wholeheartedly, to everyone who has helped me create the King's Security series. Thank you to Maria, at Steamy Designs, for your beautiful covers. They are absolute fire.

Thank you to Kate, for your work polishing each and every one of these books, and to Julie and Serena for helping me make them the best they can be.

Thank you to Dinah, for being a wonderful pair of final eyes, and to all of my Street Team and ARC readers for leaving reviews that make me smile and spreading the word about these books.

Thank you to my family and friends for your ongoing support, and especially, to my husband. Last, but certainly not least.

ABOUT THE AUTHOR

A. Rivers writes romance with strong heroes and heroines who kick butt and take names. She loves MMA fighters, private investigators, military men, bodyguards, and the protective guy next door who isn't afraid to fight the odds for love. She also writes small town romance as Alexa Rivers.